A DAN

Renata had lost three men she had loved
to the terrible Himalaya, and she was
determined never again to get involved
with a mountaineer. But then, in Kathmandu, she met Grant Fowler – and soon
realised she had met the love of her life.
But Grant hadn't told her very much
about himself ...

# A DANGEROUS PASSION

BY

JAYNE BAULING

**MILLS & BOON LIMITED**
15–16 BROOK'S MEWS
LONDON W1A 1DR

First published in Great Britain 1987
by Mills & Boon Limited

© Jayne Bauling 1987

Australian copyright 1987
Philippine copyright 1987
This edition 1987

ISBN 0 263 75667 X

Set in Times 10 on 11½ pt.
01-0587-48939

Computer typeset by SB Datagraphics,
Colchester, Essex

Printed and bound in Great Britain by
Collins, Glasgow

# CHAPTER ONE

THERE he was again.

The noise of the marketplace receded and the colourful crowds became a blur as Renata Armstrong paused inadvertently, her attention captured and held, her awareness of him so intense that it took up her entire consciousness and she didn't even notice that she had lost Karen.

She was struck less by the coincidence of seeing him again so soon, as Kathmandu was a small city and Europeans tended to stand out, than by her own complex reactions. A tiny bubble of excitement was growing, in conflict with a gathering sense of disturbance that was almost foreboding, as if in some way he threatened her.

It was strange, both exhilarating and unnerving, to find herself reacting to a man in this way after the frozen years in which she had been oblivious to all emotional and physical temptation. It was like an awakening from a long, cold sleep, and it caused a feeling of guilt as she realised what was happening to her, as if she committed a betrayal, although she had always known that her long mourning must one day ease and end, even if the bitterness of her loss never quite left her.

It was inevitable. She was young and healthy, and he was the most arrestingly male creature she had ever seen. Renata knew she was staring, but she couldn't help herself. Casual cream jeans and a dark blue shirt clad a frame that was lean but well put together, exuding an impression of controlled strength. Power was in those shoulders and the bare tanned forearms with their covering of fine dark hairs, and the dark head was carried at an angle denoting utter self-confidence and an unconscious pride. The carved profile was arrogant and his bearing was that of a man who exercised authority as a right.

Was that why she felt threatened? He was one who would command, perhaps even dominate. He would be a demanding lover——

Renata flushed slightly at discovering herself thinking of a perfect stranger in such a context, and it was as if the sensuality of her fantasising reached out and betrayed her, because it was at that moment that he turned and looked at her.

It was as it had been yesterday up at the monkey temple. Dark, stormy grey eyes assessed her with little mercy for her sudden discomfiture. It was a ruthless inspection without being hostile, and her quickened breath caught in her throat. It was a moment of panic, but also of knowledge, and she felt her blood heat at the awareness that he found her desirable.

The glimmer of a smile appeared, flickering about his mouth. It was a beautiful mouth, the mouth of a passionate lover, and the energy of his virility seemed to reach out and claim her without his even stirring from where he stood. Suddenly Renata was frightened, as much by the clamour of her rioting woman's flesh as by the way he seemed to mark her as his simply by standing there and looking at her.

It was too soon. She wasn't ready.

She thrust her shaking hands into the pockets of the vivid Nepalese patchwork jacket she wore over her jeans, while her inner muscles clamped, clenching as if to deny him ownership. With the reserve back in her deep sapphire eyes once more, she looked away from him with as much cool disdain as she could summon, aware as she did so of the flash of anger in storm-grey eyes and the tightening of his features as he marked the rejection that was a denial of the instantaneous awareness that had flared between them on both the occasions that they had stood looking at each other in crowded public places.

Yesterday afternoon it had been amid the filth and stench of the monkey temple which had been a hang-out for many Westerners, remnants of the Sixties drug culture, until 1975 when the Nepalese government had outlawed the use of drugs, including hashish, in response to a United Nations appeal. These days, many impoverished Nepalese camped there, and Renata had fallen into the habit of taking medicines for the baby of one family, although it was a secret she kept to herself, having a natural horror of being thought a do-gooder.

That first encounter had been as silent and as explicit as today's, ending similarly, and it had taken Renata hours to rid her mind of him. A thousand questions had teased her—who he was, where he came from, what he was doing in Kathmandu and even if he had a woman in his life. He had had a companion yesterday, but a man, younger than he was, with Irish blue eyes and equipped with one of the most sophisticated and expensive cameras available, which had led Renata to wonder if they were tourists. They didn't have that air, but the man, her man, had apparently been pointing out things of interest to the younger.

Today, however, he was alone, and she wondered what he was doing in the marketplace.

'What happened to you?' Her friend Karen Richards had come back for her. 'I turned round and you weren't there any more, and I'd been talking away to you.'

'Sorry, I slowed down.'

For some reason which she failed to analyse, Renata didn't want to share this, but it was expecting too much to think Karen would miss so devastating a man a second time.

'Is he sexy, or is he sexy?' Karen asked her standard question as her hazel eyes were riveted in their turn. 'What do you think, Renata?'

'I suppose so,' Renata admitted reluctantly.

'Then he must be,' Karen teased. 'Do we toss a coin or fight it out? And how can we arrange an encounter? Something more original than colliding with him?'

'Karen!' Renata laughed protestingly. 'We can't just ... pick him up. He's going anyway, and we're going the other way.'

'Pity,' sighed Karen. 'But looking like that, he's probably booked already and wouldn't look at the likes of us anyway. How old would you say he was? Mid-thirties? Not American.'

'How can you know that?'

'I can tell.' An American herself, Karen shrugged. 'The clothes or something. Talking of which, let's get on and pick up those pants. I hope they're ready.'

They made their way up a dark sloping alley and along another, between dim houses and tiny shops interspersed with ancient carved temples, being careful where they placed their feet, for livestock and a multitude of hungry dogs moved freely about the labyrinthine alleys and squares of Kathmandu. The late summer sun had sunk golden behind the rooftops, but the Nepalese people were still out in their hundreds, a handsome people whose facial features were reminiscent of Burma and Malay. Renata and Karen were known by this time, no longer mistaken for tourists, and could thus pass without too much importuning from the juvenile population, attractive black-haired children, the girls' plaits threaded with coloured ribbons, their nails scarlet and even the toddlers' eyes ringed with a kohl-like substance.

'I spoke to Alec earlier,' Karen was telling Renata. 'He suggested a farewell dinner tonight. The four of us?'

'Fine,' Renata agreed. 'Where? The Yak and Yeti again?'

'No. I was in the mood for Chinese, so it's the restaurant at the Annapurna, if that's okay with you? We'll meet there, about eight-thirty.'

Alec Lumley and Wes Davies were two young New Zealand doctors spending a couple of years working at a hospital in the Sola Khumbu region, an area of Nepal which the New Zealanders had made peculiarly their own. They occasionally visited Kathmandu for a break, and when they did so, Renata and Karen were happy to partner them, but there was no deep commitment. Renata knew that Karen slept with Alec when they were together, but they had no long-term plans for the future. Her own friendship with the quieter Wes had been purely platonic ever since his one attempt to make love to her had met with a frozen, unhappy response, and she knew he now saw a lot of a beautiful young Sherpani in one of the Sola Khumbu villages.

'They're leaving tonight, aren't they?' Renata questioned her friend.

'Yes. I'm due a few days off, as you know, so I thought I'd go with them, do some hiking and then fly back from either Lukla or the strip above Namche Bazar.'

The possibility of Renata joining her was not even mentioned. She would never go to Sola Khumbu again, although she had hiked all over the lovely Kathmandu Valley with Karen and even, once, been into the foothills, but the latter had been an unhappy experience.

The pants they had ordered from a tiny ill-lit shop in one of the alleys were ready, several pairs each in soft fabric and the colours of their choice, with drawstring waists and wide legs gathered in at the ankles.

'I'd better be making tracks for my apartment if I'm leaving with the boys,' said Karen as they left the shop. 'I still have to get my gear together. You?'

'Home for me too. There's nothing on at the Embassy this evening.'

Karen eyed her speculatively and ventured, 'I suppose they'll be planning some kind of bash for the British expedition? A reception, anyway?'

The delicate tinting that normally touched Renata's cheeks had fled, leaving her ivory-pale, making her silky dark hair look almost black in contrast, and shadows gathered swiftly in her eyes.

'Expedition?' Her voice was a dry little sound, and she could almost resent Karen for making her ask it.

'Everest,' Karen confirmed sympathetically.

'Autumn? Post-monsoon?'

'Yes.'

'I hadn't heard anything about it,' Renata said flatly.

'You wouldn't,' Karen agreed wryly.

It was an ability Renata had cultivated ruthlessly until it became a habit. To one subject and all that pertained to it, she was as deaf and blind as a corpse, obliterating anguish instead of exorcising it, so that the old bitterness lay buried along with her one-time fascination and interest.

And yet the deliberate, wilful ignorance was against everything in her nature and upbringing, and forced into awareness now, the girl whose childhood heroes had been men like Reinhold Messner and Chris Bonington instead of the usual singers and rock groups couldn't resist asking, 'Alpine—or siege-style?'

'Wouldn't know.'

'Alpine,' Renata decided, her father's daughter. 'Or semi-alpine, rather. Siege is becoming obsolete.'

'Oxygenless. I did hear that.'

'Which route?'

'South-West Face.'

But Renata's face had closed and the wariness and reserve had replaced the shadows in her eyes. You had to conceal pain, because it wasn't considerate or polite to share it with others. Tragedy embarrassed people, discomfited them.

'Don't be cross with me, Renata,' Karen said.

'I'm not really,' she replied dully. 'I just don't want to talk about it.'

'Or think about it. Four years, Renata?'

'Three men in three years,' she retorted curtly, angrily, wanting to lash out and punish her friend for forcing this on her.

'You'd have had to face it eventually,' Karen pointed out candidly. 'You've only been at the Embassy a year and in that time the British seem to have been concentrating on the other eight-thousanders, but Everest has always been a sort of British mountain, if you know what I mean.'

'More's the pity,' Renata agreed bitterly, pausing as

they came to the main road where she and Karen must part to go their different ways, both accustomed to walking everywhere in Kathmandu. 'Forget it, Karen, it's not your fault. It's not anyone's fault. There are mountains and men must climb them, but never, ever again will I let myself love one of those men. See you at eight-thirty. The Annapurna.'

Out here in the broad street, the sun still reached, spreading its late summer warmth, and Renata walked on in its last golden rays, past a large group of Gurkhas out for an evening training run, towards the little flat that had been provided for her.

It had been ironical that her first overseas posting should have been to Kathmandu, but she had never thought to lie about her knowledge of Nepali and Sherpa acquired during those years when her father had wanted to give something back to the country and people which had given him so much and had brought his entire family out to live in Nepal for a couple of years. Renata had been at the Embassy for a year now, and she still wasn't sure if her return to Nepal had helped or hindered her wounds. She liked Kathmandu, and the Himalaya were far away and invisible, and yet too close.

Everest. Sagarmatha, they called it in Nepal, and Chomolongma on the Tibetan side, and others called it The Widow Maker. It had made a widow of her mother seven years ago and three years later had taken her son from her. From Renata it had taken father and brother . . .

And her love. Ang Tsering Lama.

Of course, there were other peaks, and other ranges even, that had trimmed the list of friends and acquaintances, but as Karen had said, Everest was a 'British' mountain and the years had taken a cruel toll, from way back in 1924 with the loss of Mallory and Irvine on the Tibetan side, to all those other famous post-war names, like Burke and Boardman and Tasker, and among them Stephen Armstrong and Darryl Armstrong.

And Ang Tsering Lama among the Sherpa names.

Her mind went back to the little information Karen had given her regarding the forthcoming British expedition. She no longer knew any mountaineers, having cut herself off from their world entirely; she didn't know who the new men were, nor which of the old still lived and climbed; but still she shivered despite the warmth of the evening and her jacket, too well informed to dismiss the risks. The South-West Face, like the original south col route, meant the Ice Fall, from which her father's body had never been recovered, buried beneath the icy debris of a giant serac, as if the gods mocked his successful ascent of a couple of days before by the old Hillary route.

She did not know how the other two had died, three years later, high on the west ridge. The bitterness she had not felt at sixteen with her father's loss had overflowed with their disappearance. She had not wanted to know, refusing to listen. They were dead and she didn't even have their bodies back. The mountain had taken those too, lifeless and broken, and returned her nothing.

Never again, she had sworn at nineteen, bereft of all the men she had ever loved. Never again, she had vowed when she returned to England and saw her mother's face.

Her mother had been appalled when Renata had been posted to Nepal, and angry with her for accepting the posting; her older sister Janine had found more favour, peacefully married to a Shropshire estate agent; she now lived for her grandchildren, and please God the little boy never wanted to climb, because how could you stop him if the compulsion was there?

Letting herself into her flat with its bright, simple décor of local furniture and fabrics, Renata removed her jacket and got herself a bowl of yoghurt, then wandered about feeling oddly helpless. She supposed it was the result of being knocked off balance twice in one day, first by the man in the marketplace and then by Karen's news of a British expedition.

Finally, she went into her bedroom and got out the framed photo she kept in her bedside drawer, although whether guilt or sadness prompted her, she was unsure.

She sat on the edge of her bed, the photo in her hands. The face that looked out at her was young and vibrant with the handsome features of the Sherpas, the eyes bright with laughter, the smile somehow both gentle and mischievous.

Ang Tsering Lama had been just twenty-four when he died. One of a new generation of Sherpas, he had been educated at one of the Hillary schools, spoke several languages fluently and had been to America.

Renata had been spending her university vacation in Nepal because her brother was a member of an expedition attempting Everest. Having served as a much valued Ice Fall Sherpa for the Austrians the previous autumn, followed by a complete spring ascent of Cho Oyu, the world's eighth highest peak, Ang Tsering had been recommended as a high-altitude Sherpa. He had been ambitious to go high, to rank along with Tanzing, Pasang and Pertemba, and the leader of the expedition had promised him a place in one of the summit pairs despite his youth.

'I want to go high,' he had explained during the acclimatising trek through Sola Khumbu which Renata had been given permission to join. 'I want to go as high as it's possible for a man to go.'

Their love had grown swiftly, with no room for doubts, and there had been nothing in the way of a culture clash since he was very Westernised, while Renata knew his country and its people almost as well as she did her own.

'We'll announce our engagement when I get back,' he had promised when they had agreed they wanted marriage. 'But first I want to get to the top. It will be my engagement present to you; I'll dedicate it to you.'

But he hadn't come back, and neither had her brother. The news had been brought to her where she awaited them in a little pre-fabricated hut at Thyangboche to which she had returned when the time the government was permitting them to spend on the mountain was almost at its end.

Ang Tsering Lama and Darryl Armstrong would never come back, and Renata would never come there again.

She stirred now, realising that the light had faded while she sat with her memories, so that even his happy, confident image was taken from her. Slowly she replaced the photo in its drawer and began to move through the flat, closing curtains and switching on lights.

It might be that the time had come to let go at last. Her reaction to the man in the marketplace seemed to indicate that she was ready.

She would always mourn them, but the grief of her loss would stab less sharply and it would not be betrayal. What would always remain acute and agonising, however, would be the bitterness of the suspicion—no, of the knowledge that those three men, and others like them, had loved the game more than they did the women in their lives, wives, mothers, daughters, sisters, sweet-hearts and lovers.

That, more than any other reason, was why she had vowed—never again. Never another mountain man. The mountains were a rival unlike any other, not to be challenged, and the power they exercised over those men who had succumbed to their temptation was absolute and unassailable, more than any woman could wield.

She would never accept the mountains as her rival again. Another woman she could and would fight, but not the mountains. That was why she had severed all ties with the mountaineering fraternity.

It was still early, so she had plenty of time to prepare to meet Karen and the two doctors at the Annapurna; too much time in a way, she realised, finding the flat a lonely place tonight. She was glad she was going out, glad that she had a few friends outside the Embassy where, at twenty-three, she was very much the staff baby, just as Karen was at the American Embassy.

She needed people again, she realised, and wondered when that had started.

She had been frozen in her long grief, but now . . . The man in the marketplace had shown her that the thaw was begun.

The man. He filled her thoughts while she bathed and dressed. Meeting her own eyes in the mirror, Renata flushed, for they were darkened, hot and disturbed, as she realised she had been fantasising about him again, both as a lover and love, not just as a bedmate but as a daily companion too, a lifetime partner.

And she would probably never set eyes on him again! Somehow, though, she couldn't help believing that she would, as if it were destined that way. Impatiently she tried to mock herself out of so wild a fancy, but the conviction persisted.

She was slightly stunned and embarrassed by what had happened to her. He was a total stranger, whose name and nationality she didn't know, and yet he obsessed her. She hadn't expected it to be this way. She had been wrong, in fact. It was no slow, gradual thaw that he had started, but a swift, hot melting, its effects as devastating as an avalanche.

She was dressed in one of the new pairs of pants, subtle off-white, after finding she had a suitable top, heavy silk in the same colour, and hoped she would be warm enough. The weather was unpredictable at this time of year, and today had been unusually cool and clear. She and Karen generally dressed casually for their dates with the two doctors, but she took the trouble to make up, apply perfume, and her straight dark hair, just shorter than shoulder-length, she drew back and up on one side with a mother-of-pearl clasp. Finally she decided that this style of pants demanded high heels. She would treat herself to a taxi for once.

Karen met her at the hotel and they went to the bar to wait for the men, unsurprised by their absence. Wes and Alec had hundreds of friends and acquaintances who all seemed to end up in Nepal eventually, and they were frequently delayed by meeting up with them.

'Alec swears they're models of punctuality at the hospital,' laughed Karen as she started a second glass of the sweetish local gin and lime.

'I suppose the way they break out in Kathmandu is a reaction to the self-discipline required there,' Renata agreed.

Eventually the men arrived and they went across to the Chinese restaurant, beautifully decorated and with the lights kept comfortably low. Renata looked at them, sitting opposite her and Karen who had their backs to the wall: two bearded men who lived life to the full without inhibitions or hang-ups, qualities that made them ideal companions. At present they were joking with the waiter about how hungry they always felt after a Chinese meal, and Renata laughed. She preferred Nepalese food herself, well curried, but Karen was a dim sum addict.

They were good friends to have, these three people, she reflected gratefully. They made no heavy demands, were easy-going and light-hearted without being superficial, and she realised how much lonelier her life would have been without them. She looked at Wes Davies, his deep brown eyes startling in contrast to the fairness of his hair and beard, and she smiled. Theirs was in a sense a symbiotic relationship, each of them preventing the other from feeling *de trop* with the other two, although she doubted if either Alec or Karen would have minded being a threesome instead of a foursome. They enjoyed each other, but they weren't in love.

Something, a feeling of being compelled as if by some magnetic force, made her look up—and there he was again, the man from the marketplace, striding across the restaurant in a light-coloured shirt and tight dark jeans. For a moment grey eyes glanced her way, smouldered, flashed and were withdrawn.

Renata sat very still, half terrified, while another part of her wanted to laugh. This was too much. Coincidence or fate?

The men with their backs to the room were still

absorbed in exchanging repartee with their waiter, but Karen had seen.

'What a bod!' she murmured wickedly for Renata's ears alone. 'He looked at you, did you notice?'

'Yes. Don't tease—please, Karen,' she begged, and Karen kindly refrained.

Perhaps she took life too seriously, Renata reflected wryly, but she couldn't bring herself to joke about it. She had been shattered anew by the impact of that stormy glance and electric presence, and somehow it was an intensely personal thing, not for sharing. It was all happening so fast, and yet nothing was really happening, and perhaps it never would. They might go on seeing each other all over the place and never meeting, and perhaps it would be safer that way. He frightened her, or rather her reaction to him frightened her. It was so intense, overwhelming, and she had never felt like this before. It made her feel a stranger to herself, with no control over her reactions.

Their meal was served, and Renata couldn't help glancing towards the man's table every so often, and speculating about him. He had another man with him tonight, not the young man from the monkey temple. She wondered if he was staying at the Annapurna, or just dining here. He could be a businessman, since he appeared to have no female companion and yet was very definitely, blatantly, heterosexual. She knew a lot of businessmen chose this hotel when in Nepal.

What if he was married? What if they didn't speak each other's languages? Only they had held two conversations already, without the use of words, she reminded herself, before deciding she was going crazy. Here she was, panicking about all sorts of things, and all because of a stranger!

But they must meet! Suddenly she wanted that more than she had wanted anything in a long, long time. Next time he looked at her with that flickering half-smile, she mustn't take fright and turn her gaze away as she had this afternoon. She must—Renata felt her cheeks grow warm as the phrase 'green light' drifted across her mind. She was anticipating behaviour in which she had never before indulged and of which her mother would most definitely disapprove, although she knew Janine would applaud.

The meal was an extended affair because Wes and Alec were in high spirits, but eventually Wes said, 'We ought to get going if we've still got to pick up Karen's gear. Pity you aren't coming with us, Ren. Do you want to share our taxi?'

This was the moment of decision. Renata glanced towards the table where her man sat and saw that his companion had left. A host of butterflies invaded her stomach. He was waiting for her . . .

She smiled at her friends as they stood up. 'Thanks, but I'll get them to bring me a last gin and lime from the bar and then make my own way home.'

Karen hung back after goodbyes had been said and the men were handing out tips they probably couldn't afford, since they were habitually broke.

'Shrewd move, Renata, getting all the action to yourself. Why did I decide to go with the boys? Not that I'd have much chance. It's you he's been watching all night—and Wes. I think he was contemplating beating Wes to a pulp. Make sure he's not some sort of maniac, and if he's married or keeps talking about his mother, forget it!'

'Karen,' Renata laughed faintly. 'His mother! He doesn't . . . he doesn't——'

'Look as if he's of woman born,' Karen supplied. 'More like Made on Olympus. Take care, babe.'

What was she doing, behaving like this? Renata wondered frantically, stifling an impulse to run after the others, and ordering a drink from the waiter who came to see why she was still there.

He was still watching her, broodingly, and—— Oh, God, suppose he really was some kind of maniac, or a con-man or a spy or a terrorist! He could know she was from the Embassy . .

Then he smiled at her, a proper smile this time, which lit his entire face and made him even more devastatingly attractive than she had realised, and this time Renata smiled back, shyly and shakily, it was true, but he could read the signal.

Her heart was thundering and she couldn't breathe properly as she watched him come across to her table with a lithe, economical walk.

'This is a pick-up,' he announced in an attractive voice that could only be English, and she smiled again as he sat down opposite her. 'I've been trying to think of an alternative way, but I don't think we've any mutual friends to introduce us and . . . we had to meet, didn't we? Grant Fowler.'

'Renata Armstrong,' she breathed.

'Can I order you a drink?'

'I've already ordered one.'

'You live here, don't you? I heard you speaking Nepali to that family at the monkey temple.' The dark grey eyes caressed her face and Renata shook because it felt as if he actually touched her.

'I'm at the British Embassy,' she explained.

'What do you do there?'

'I . . .' She paused, looking at him assessingly, and he laughed, an attractive sound that made her shiver again.

'It's all right, truly, but I respect your professional discretion. At this early stage,' he added deliberately.

It was a question, a request for confirmation, but Renata couldn't give it yet. She was still nervous, and shocked by the way she was falling apart under the impact of his personality and sensuality. It was as if they had entered a field of electricity. The atmosphere was tense, alive and quivering with some sort of excitement, on the verge of exploding into something incandescent, wonderful and terrifying.

She said lightly, 'It's not a very important job, really. What about you?'

'What about me?'

Reluctantly, it seemed, he withdrew his attention from her as the waiter arrived with her drink and he ordered something for himself before looking at her again.

'What do you do? Why are you here?' she elaborated.

He looked at her contemplatively, eyes a little reserved for once, and then he smiled slightly. 'Let's put it this way: I have various business interests and I travel a lot.'

Renata looked back at him thoughtfully. 'That's not a very full answer, but then I didn't give you one either. I suppose you're a millionaire.'

He laughed then. 'No, but I'm rich.'

'That's a nice plain word. Most people say well-off or comfortable. Where do you live?'

'I've got a place in London at the moment, but, as I say, I travel extensively.'

'Toilet seats?'

He looked startled and then smiled. 'No. Is it a riddle? Explain it to me.'

She laughed. 'I wondered if you were embarrassed by your business, since you obviously don't want to elaborate. I once met a man, right here in the Annapurna, who was a toilet seat salesman. He said it was as good a way of seeing the world as any, and he'd been absolutely everywhere.'

His eyes had darkened. 'Who was he?'

'I don't know,' Renata protested. 'I don't think he even told me his name or gave me his card or anything. He knew I wasn't a potential customer.'

'He wasn't a boy-friend or lover, then?'

She stared at him and then challenged quietly, 'And do I come here often? Quite often, Mr Fowler, but I don't do this sort of thing often. In fact, I never have before and maybe I shouldn't have done it tonight, if——'

'I'm sorry,' he apologised swiftly and charmingly. 'And it's not Mr Fowler, Renata, it's Grant. Who was the young man with you tonight, the blond one sitting opposite you? Not the toilet seat salesman, I take it.'

Renata's eyes began to sparkle and her lips curved as she realised what lay behind his questioning. 'That's my friend Wes Davies. They're all my friends. The men are New Zealand doctors doing a couple of years here—in Sola Khumbu—and Karen is from the U.S. Embassy.'

'What sort of friend?'

'A friend-friend. Can I interrogate you now?'

The man's moody, passionate nature was evident in the way he looked at her for a few moments, eyes smouldering with angry doubt, his mouth harsh, but gradually he relaxed, smiling. 'What do you want to know?'

'Everything,' she claimed extravagantly, then blushed.

'There'll be time enough for that,' he assured her confidently.

Hurriedly, she asked, 'Where's your friend? The one who was with you at the monkey temple? Blue eyes and a camera.'

Instantly, he was brooding again, and she was sorry because she hadn't done it intentionally, merely asking the first question that occurred to her.

'Why are you interested?'

'I'm not. Really.'

'You noticed his eyes.'

'Who wouldn't?' she retorted, adding laughingly, 'Stop it, Grant!'

He looked surprised before smiling reluctantly. 'I'm behaving badly, aren't I? But I want you to ask questions about me, not Pat who, incidentally, is doing the tourist bit as this is his first visit, and has gone to watch the Nepalese dancing at the hall down the road.'

Renata smiled. 'Thank you. All right, about you! Married? Are you now or have you ever been?'

'No, and no. When I am, it will be permanently.'

'I can tell you'll be a very possessive husband,' she taunted gently.

'Yes, I'm afraid so,' he sighed. 'And you, Renata? What sort of wife will you be?'

# CHAPTER TWO

RENATA stared at Grant, knowing by both his tone and look that he meant it personally. He meant what sort of a wife would she be to him?

She laughed a little breathlessly. 'This is crazy!'

'No,' he stated arrogantly. 'Don't be coy about it, Renata. We both know what's happening here, between the two of us. We both know we're going to be lovers and probably married.' She felt as if the last breath had been knocked from her lungs and her stomach flipped nervously.

'Don't,' she said, barely above a whisper. 'It's too far, too fast, already.'

'I won't rush you,' he promised. 'But it's happening, and you'd be a fool to deny it.'

'I can't handle it!'

Sheer terror gripped her. It was too strange, too sudden, and to hear it put into words made it too real as well. Her whole identity was threatened. He had drawn her into an alien world, without even having touched her, a world dark and glittering with the promise of passion and the threat of some sort of bondage, both physical and emotional. Temptation and fear were equal, and suddenly she needed to escape, before she lost all that was safe and familiar in herself.

The old love was a temporary refuge, a cocoon, but Grant Fowler's dark magnetic power reached her even there in that safe, sacred haven. She thought of Ang

Tsering Lama, of the gentle warmth of their unconsummated love, but she was looking at Grant Fowler, quivering and helpless under the dominance of his stormy, restless gaze, and his words dragged her roughly out into the danger of reality again:

'Why can't you handle it?' he demanded.

'You'll smother me, take me over, try to own me.' Renata couldn't dissemble at that moment. 'You've admitted that you're possessive, and you're already doing it, trying to own me ... my soul, even.'

He smiled. 'It's your body I'm interested in at the moment, but stop panicking, Renata. It won't be yet. There are things I need to know first, to be sure of ... You have a tragic mouth when you aren't smiling, and there's almost always an element of reserve in your eyes, and you're not going to tell me, are you? You aren't going to tell me what put them there, so I'll have to banish them.'

'You see, you're still doing it,' she whispered, eyes dark with fear and resentment. 'Not just taking me over, but making me over, trying to drive out my secrets and change my nature. I have a history, a past life, everyone does. You can't take that away and make me into someone brand new who never thought or felt before.'

'I wish I could.' But the dark words were followed by a lightning change of mood as he laughed. 'God, I'm doing a good job of scaring you off, talking like a madman! I didn't realise until tonight that possessiveness was a fault of mine ... No, and it damn well wasn't until now. It's your doing, Renata, so perhaps you can cure it too, but until I'm sure of you, I'm jealous of everyone and everything you've ever cared about, every experience that has shaped and influenced you ... But you're wrong about one thing. I don't want to take away your history, whatever it is. You wouldn't be you without it.'

The last sentence was almost gently spoken, and Renata was touched. She said softly, 'Then be patient, Grant. You're not the only one who needs to be sure. I'm not ... very experienced, but isn't all this pretty ... heavy, for a first meeting?'

'Not when we know what we both know,' he retorted sardonically. 'That cuts away the conventionalities, doesn't it? But in deference to your inexperience— which, incidentally, is one of the best things I've learned about you tonight—we can return to superficial topics, especially as I'm genuinely curious as to why you were delivering patent medicines to that family squatting up at the monkey temple.'

Embarrassed, Renata looked down into her untouched drink. 'Oh, it's just that the baby is always sick ... It's inevitable, living in those conditions, and they won't move, so it's all I can do, really. You know, when I arrived a year ago, I went to visit the Tibetan refugee camp here. Do you know it? They're exiles from their home, of course, but apart from that tragedy, their living conditions are better than those of most of the local people because their plight is publicised around the world and aid pours in.'

She felt more at ease now that the subject was impersonal, and she listened to Grant's responses and opinions with interest, realising from the depth of his knowledge that this could not be his first visit to Nepal. Her fascination grew. He spoke entertainingly, with humour and intelligence, and he was interested in her thoughts and ideas, encouraging her to express herself. She was surprised when finally she looked at her watch, since the waiters seemed to be hovering, to discover that they had been talking for well over an hour, and they had hardly touched their drinks.

She sighed, smiling ruefully as he looked at her questioningly. 'Grant, I must go now, truly.'

'Where do you live? I've hired a car while I'm here, so I'll drive you home.'

Momentarily, her heart leapt because if he had hired a car it must mean he was remaining in Nepal for some time. But then all her nervousness and uncertainty at finding herself so unexpectedly involved with this man came flooding back and she looked at him with eyes dark with apprehension.

'It's all right, I can get a taxi.' She sipped a little of her drink because her mouth was suddenly dry.

'I said I wouldn't rush you, Renata,' he reminded her gently. 'I just want to take you home, see where you live. Finish your drink if you want it and we'll go.'

Still nervous and yet not really wanting to lose his company just yet, she yielded silently.

It was a short drive to the block housing her flat, and now they were both silent. Renata was tense, excited and fearful all at the same time, and attempting some sort of analysis, she supposed she was still off balance after the shock of her reaction to this man plus her own uncharacteristic behaviour in actually encouraging him.

She was violently attracted to him, she admitted, as he obviously was to her, but was it possible that she had also fallen in love with him in the space of little more than an hour? Not even the discovery that he was a moody man with a tendency towards possessiveness had done anything to lessen this fatal fascination ... Oh, dear God, he must give her time and space.

But would he? He had already told her that they would be lovers, and perhaps even man and wife. That he wasn't someone who bothered much with the conventions, and she suspected he was an impatient man who would go directly to the heart of any matter rather than indulge in ritual circumlocution.

She glanced at his profile, oddly remote now that his attention was on the road rather than her, and realised with some surprise that he had not once actually touched her yet. How strange, when she felt as if he had. Her flesh had burned every time he looked at her, as if he branded her with those hot, darkly grey eyes, marking her as his property.

That was what she was so afraid of, she reflected. She wasn't afraid of loving again, after four years' mourning, but she didn't want to be merely a man's property, owned and possessed and, wilful and tempestuous, Grant Fowler was a man who would want to dominate. She doubted if even a stronger-minded woman than she could resist him.

Her flat was on the second floor of a three-storey block, squat but attractive, in a clean, pleasant area where the streets were wide and fairly quiet at most times, particularly at this hour of night.

'Nice building,' commented Grant as he parked the hired car outside.

'Yes, it's old, but it was completely renovated just before I came to Kathmandu. They even put in a lift, and the security is good; the lobby is never unattended and there are regular and thorough patrols of the entire building, including fire escapes.' She was talking nervously, trying to find a way of saying goodnight. Finally, she omitted all embellishments. 'Goodnight.'

'Will you let me come in with you?' he asked quietly.

'Grant . . .'

'I've promised you, no more than you want,' he went on. 'Trust me, Renata.'

'I . . .'

'Please!' Suddenly his tone was urgent.

'All right,' she yielded, somewhere between sighing and laughing, knowing herself for a fool, but the appeal in his voice had been irresistible.

'Anyway, you still haven't told me where I can contact you,' he went on more calmly when the lift was carrying them up to her floor.

'At the Embassy during the day.'

'And do you have a phone here?'

'Yes.' She preceded him out of the lift. 'Grant——'

'I've got a few things to organise, but otherwise I want to spend as much time as possible with you,' he went on. 'With a bit of rearranging, I can probably manage more free time.'

Wondering what his business could be, that he had been so reluctant to talk about it, Renata opened her flat door, going into the lounge, putting down her bag and switching on the two lamps.

'Coffee?' she asked, turning to look at him.

'No, nothing, thanks.' He paused, glancing round the little lounge which she had made attractive with small touches of her own, soft pashmina shawls in neutral colours over the couch, a vase of wild cosmos in white and shades of pink and mauve gathered in the countryside a few days ago when she and Karen had hired bicycles and gone cycling through Kathmandu Valley. Then Grant looked at her again as he took a small diary from his pocket. 'What's your number here?'

She gave it to him and then asked awkwardly, 'Won't you . . . sit down?'

But he stood where he was, a tall man radiating vitality, sexual energy and a power that was as much mental as physical, too much for this small lounge of hers, too much for her, so that she felt oppressed, panicky.

'Does it bother you that I'm here?' he asked quietly, reading her look.

'Yes,' she said faintly, her smile wobbly.

'Why?'

'I feel . . . invaded. My peace, my privacy,' she elaborated candidly. 'It's too . . . soon.'

'Yes.' His face was dark now, expressionless for once, but there was a deep, incomprehensible glow in those incredible eyes. 'Tell me, Renata, am I making a hell of a fool of myself?'

The moment of uncertainty in a man so arrogantly sure of himself was startling, but it was the fact that he refused to conceal it that stirred her as nothing else had done and she realised that in a sense it was typical of him. There was a kind of pride in honesty, and he was a proud man.

She laughed shakily. 'If you are, then so am I.'

'So we'll be fools together.'

'But . . . not yet,' she qualified quietly, not denying it.

'No, not yet,' Grant agreed curtly, his face now taut with strain and the tension between them intensified to an unbearable pitch, a live quivering atmosphere that the slightest additional disturbance could detonate. 'That's why I'm leaving now. I'll ring you.'

'Yes,' Renata whispered, held in thrall by the living

current of sexual attraction that linked them, so barely controlled now.

But still he made no move, just standing there looking at her and finally saying slowly, 'I want you. I want you and I haven't even touched you yet.'

'Grant . . .' Renata's mouth was dry, her heart racing beneath her ribs.

His voice roughened. 'Ah, God, Renata, I must at least hold you and kiss you, just once, and find out if you feel in my arms the way I've imagined since I first saw you.'

But would it stop there?

It was the last thought that occurred to her before she went up in flames, taken into his arms. Her head was level with his shoulders and Grant bent to her as she cried out, less in protest or fear than in shock at the instantaneous reaction of her senses to his touch as desire burst rampant through the bonds of self-control.

An odd, strangled sound of relief escaped Grant as their lips touched for the first time, and then he was possessing her mouth, invasive tongue fiercely passionate in exploring the soft flesh, caressing it. Trembling, Renata slid her arms up to encircle his neck, her fingers burying themselves convulsively in his dark hair as pleasure leapt, stoked by the erotic choreography created by their lips and tongues.

There was a dull roaring in Renata's ears and she was bereft of all coherent thought, responding mindlessly to the deep, driving sensuality of Grant's kiss. Heat flooded her body, her breasts were filling with hot blood, hardening and swelling, and her hips jerked and quivered against him. Strong, sure hands slid compulsively to her hips and buttocks, drawing her up hard against the throbbing bulk of his full arousal, and Renata whimpered softly in the back of her throat, arching tautly, wildly out of control.

Pausing, Grant covered her face with a series of kisses, her eyelids, her brow, the bridge of her nose, before turning to the pulsing lure of her hot swollen mouth. He was inexorable, demanding a response which Renata had no wish or ability to deny him, lost as she was in a world of fiery, shimmering passion such as she had never known before. Her hands slid feverishly down over his back as their bodies strained together, fingers freeing his shirt from his belt, and then they were in contact with bare, muscled flesh, warm and slightly damp. He shuddered, groaning, at her caresses and moved her towards the couch with its soft draping of pashmina, collapsing with her into its comfort, mouth still locked to hers.

Now, moaning, she tore frantically at his shirt buttons, and he raised his head to look down into her flushed face, his eyes dark and glittering, stormy with passion, his mouth curved with harsh sensuality.

'Oh, God, I want you so badly, more than I've ever wanted anyone,' he claimed with rough urgency. 'Kissing isn't enough, is it?'

The unevenness of his tone excited her, making her inward quivering deepen to a pulsing ache, but she couldn't answer him save to murmur his name over and over again. They were a wild tangle of limbs now, desperately seeking to discover more of each other. Renata's breath came in long shuddering sobs as she caressed his hair-roughened chest, fingertips returning irresistibly to his nipples until a spasm of pleasure racked him and, as out of control as she, he gathered her convulsively close to him once more, his mouth hot and hungry at the hollow of her throat. Her hands trapped between them, Renata's fingers had a life of their own, tugging at his body hair, smoothing it, kneading the hard flesh, stroking, massaging in tiny circular movements . . .

'Grant!' she gasped protestingly as he drew back, then strove to assist him with the tiny mother-of-pearl buttons of her blouse. 'Touch me too. Please!'

With a hoarse groan, he pulled at the front fastening of her bra, almost ripping it away from her breasts, and now he was gathering her in to his side, his hands sliding up from her ribs to the taut mounds, lightly crushing them, massaging, before his fingers plucked tormentingly at her swollen nipples and she cried out in an excess of ungovernable pleasure. His mouth was sliding moistly over one silken shoulder, his breathing harsh and laboured as he dragged shuddering breaths into his lungs.

'You're beautiful, so beautiful,' he muttered thickly. 'I knew you would be.'

He pushed her back against the couch, fingers still kneading at her breasts until his mouth claimed their aching tumescence. She gasped as his tongue struck at one tender nipple and then the other, again and again, and her fingers dug into his shoulders, nails biting into his flesh as the hot, swirling sensation in her loins exploded in a molten clamour. With a harsh sound that was part satisfaction, part protest against his own need, Grant took a nipple fully into his mouth, sucking at it, massaging it with the moist roughness of his tongue, the abrasive friction making pleasure almost pain, then soothing, now inciting again, until Renata could no longer restrain her little cries of mounting desire. There was a pause, a loss, and then she felt the lash of his tongue at the other nipple, and the ecstasy of it was too much, too overwhelming, almost frightening, so that she tried to push him away in the sudden panic of inexperience, fearful of the unfolding mysteries of this world of passion into which he was initiating her.

But he mastered her easily, the dominar. male conquering by strength and the inflicting of pleasure, and she moaned in surrender as his teeth tugged gently at the fiery, throbbing peak and her secret untouched womanhood pulsed urgently as she writhed and twisted against him in the instinctive circular motion that invited his possession.

He drew back to deal with the tie of her Nepalese pants, and for Renata it was a moment of cold sanity because she opened her eyes and looked up into the face of a stranger, dark and harsh and intent. A stranger, and perhaps a new love, but the exotic features of the old suddenly swam into her mind, golden-brown face alight with love, eyes tender and warm and happy as he kissed her, never feverishly burning as this man's were.

'Not yet,' she gasped, and yet she experienced a pang of compunction as she tried to push Grant away. 'You promised——'

'Renata——' His voice was agonised, and impatient too.

'You promised you'd give me time,' she reminded him, wriggling away from him and pulling one of the pashmina shawls about her because it seemed too much effort to sort out her bra and shirt at this moment.

'Time for what?' Grant asked tautly. 'From the way things were proceeding, I would have said neither of us needed any time. You're ready for me now, Renata. Let me prove it to you.'

He was reaching for her, but something stayed him,

perhaps her sharp protest or the anxiety in her young face, and he allowed her to move out of reach.

'Don't you understand?' she pleaded nervously. 'I need time to . . . to adjust to all this. It's happening, it's a fact, I accept that, but Grant, it's so . . . I haven't been expecting anything like this, anything so . . . so——'

'So intense and all-consuming,' he supplied grimly. 'I hadn't been expecting it either, I admit. It has come as a shock to me too, so I do understand how you're feeling, Renata . . . And I did promise you time, didn't I?'

'Yes.' She smiled shakily at the reluctance with which he conceded it and added tentatively, 'Grant, maybe you should go now.'

'Definitely I should go now,' he concurred sardonically. 'Since I'm very much a flesh and blood man at this moment, and you excite me more than any woman I've ever known.'

'You excite me too,' she admitted shyly.

His eyes darkened, but he stood up, buttoning his shirt, tucking it into his belt and feeling his pockets to see if anything had been lost during their tempestuous lovemaking.

'We'll be good together,' he promised her deeply. 'Don't make me wait too long, Renata. I want a full commitment from you before I have to leave Kathmandu, so that I'll know where I stand when I return. I'll ring you tomorrow.'

'Yes.' Keeping the shawl wrapped about her, she stood up and followed him out to the tiny hall.

There, at the door, he turned to her, taking her face between his hands and staring into her eyes which grew deeply disturbed at this renewal of physical contact as she felt her nipples stiffening again and the deep secret heart of her femininity quivered with the need to embrace his maleness.

'Don't make any more dates with your Kiwi doctor,' he adjured harshly. 'You're mine now, you belong to me.'

'Possessive!' she taunted gently, standing very still, but it required considerable strength of will not to move her body against his.

'You don't like it, do you?' He frowned. 'Why not, Renata? I'm equally yours, you know. It's an equal thing. Promise me you won't see him again.'

'Why do you need promises?' she challenged softly. 'Can't you trust me    after what's happened tonight? You must know, I must have shown you——'

'Don't play with me, Renata!' Grant was imperative. 'I don't know if I can or not. There's still that reserve in your eyes. It's there now, and it was there when you suddenly decided to call a halt just now. I don't like it.'

'I promise,' she relented. 'Anyway, Wes was going back to Sola Khumbu and won't be coming through to Kathmandu for some time. Plus, he's got a Sherpani girl-friend there. Satisfied?'

'I suppose I'll have to be,' he said, with a reluctant smile for his own jealousy. Then he dropped a hard kiss on her mouth and a hot, feverish shivering began all over her body. 'You belong to me, just remember that.'

Then he was gone, and Renata locked the door and slid the security chain into place, still feeling the hard, hot imprint of his mouth on hers, like a brand that marked her as his, and she had little doubt that he had intended it as such.

A faint, rueful laugh escaped her and she leaned her head against the door for a moment. She must be in love with Grant, or she would never have been able to accept such possessiveness. But was it possible? Did people fall in love so quickly?

Still thinking about it, Renata returned to the lounge, but only to stand in the centre of the room, her face thoughtful as she tried to sort out her feelings. Of course, Grant hadn't mentioned love, but then he could be as incredulous as she and equally reluctant to raise it as a subject so ridiculously early in their relationship. Being realistic, she allowed that such possessiveness as he had evinced could be entirely sexual, but on the other hand, he had mentioned the possibility of their one day marrying earlier that evening before he had even touched her. Men didn't marry for sex alone.

Additionally, he had said something about leaving Kathmandu and then returning—to her or for her. She assumed that was what he had meant, and he had been speaking of a commitment, so at least she could be reasonably sure that he wasn't contemplating just a casual, short-term affair.

Oh, dear God, she hoped whatever it was that lay between them was truly as equal as he had said, because she was very much afraid that she was in love with him, incredible as it seemed after such brief acquaintance.

Deciding to shower, she went to the bathroom and there, for the first time, the first prick of shame assailed her after she had stripped and caught sight of her reflection in the full mirror that occupied the wall above the basin. Her mouth was swollen and blurred from Grant's kisses, her nipples still inflamed, stinging and sensitive from their first acquaintance with a man's passion, and filling once more as she relived the things his hands and mouth had done.

He had been a virtual stranger, for pity's sake! She

turned away, hastily turning on the hot tap so that the steam would mist and blur her shamed reflection.

When she entered her bedroom a little later, she couldn't help a guilty glance at the drawer which held the photo she had spent time in contemplating several hours previously.

'He would want you to be happy.' Janine had encouraged her with platitudes four years ago when she had returned to England and university, trying to persuade her to go out with one of the several young men who asked her.

Renata had known it was true; platitudes usually were; but the difficulty lay in herself. You didn't stop loving someone just because they were dead.

Now, however, her life had changed dramatically. It was time for letting go, for saying farewell and accepting that there was a new man in her life, as different as it was possible to be from the old, but to be welcomed nevertheless, because she was alive again, her heart and her body vibrant with feeling.

If only Grant gave her time. She could accept it, but she must have time. It had happened too swiftly and too overwhelmingly, utterly unexpected, and she had never dreamed that any man could make her react with quite such shattering intensity.

She needed time, and yet lying in her bed in the darkness, sensing that the edge of the monsoon was back after a day's respite, her body was ready for him now, if her heart and mind were not. The hollowness of her unsatisfied womanhood was a deep ache that made her stir fretfully, unable to find sleep. She was twenty-three and she had never known a man's possession, but she knew what she wanted. She wanted Grant Fowler; she

wanted him on her, in her, filling her with the virile
potency of his masculinity.

Eventually she slept, and in the morning the sky above
Kathmandu was hidden behind a grey canopy which
wept occasionally and never lifted, and the blanketing
effect of the cloud made Kathmandu a sweltering
cauldron.

They must have wondered at her behaviour at the
Embassy that morning; the way she dreamed over her
word processor, missed something important on the telex
and tensed every time her phone rang.

It was shortly before noon when Grant was finally put
through to her ...

In the few days that followed, they saw as much of
each other as her job and his business permitted, and
gradually Renata found herself relaxing in her mind,
even as the sexual tension between them increased, but
she still wasn't quite ready to accept him as a lover, so
though they went everywhere else, they spent no time at
her flat or his hotel.

The tiny mountain kingdom of Nepal was a country
for walking, for being outdoors, even when the last of the
monsoon clouds hung lowering overhead, and together
Renata and Grant went everywhere, not just in
Kathmandu, but throughout the valley. Familiar as
Nepal was to her, and as beloved as her own country, she
found herself appreciating it anew, as Grant admitted he
too did, because they were sharing it with each other.

It was an old-fashioned country, only opened to
outsiders in 1949, suttee only outlawed in the fifties,
although some areas had been spoilt during the days
when drugs were legal and young Westerners flocked to
what they saw as a paradise. There were still some

ageing, fading flower children to be seen about, cheeks sunken after years of opium addiction, and of course the Hari Krishna temple had kept many of its converts.

But essentially it remained as it must always have been, a country where ninety per cent of the people were Hindu and had their own sacred river which ultimately flowed into the Ganges; the rest were mostly Buddhist or Muslim, the Sherpas practising Tibetan Buddhism.

It was a country of carved temples, stupas, prayer wheels, Durbar squares; of Gurkhas holding hands with each other, and of beautiful children.

One of the most beautiful was Hamir, and Renata had to laugh when she introduced him to Grant early one evening. At only five, Hamir was cleaner and better dressed than many of the children, son of a poor, proud and hardworking family, and he never, ever begged. He was possessed of an insatiable curiosity about the world beyond Nepal's borders and school alone couldn't teach him fast enough.

That was how Renata had first met him, as he was in the habit of marching up to foreigners and firing one-word questions at them.

'Country?' he would demand with his angelic smile, and if the answer was new to him, 'Capital?'

Now he looked up at Grant and having asked for his country turned to Renata and enquired, 'Husband?'

Renata laughed, thinking he and Grant had something in common despite the difference in their sizes. They both came straight to the point, never wasting any breath.

But Grant looked down at Hamir with an oddly indulgent smile and said simply, 'Not yet.'

It was just one more incident that added to the

reassurance that Renata needed, and it was increasing all
the time. It was real, he meant it, she thought as they said
goodbye to Hamir and moved on, and tiny bubbles of
warmth and excitement rose inside her.

She smiled at Grant. 'Do you know where you're
making for, or are we just walking?'

'I heard this morning that they've installed a new
living goddess since I was last here, and I want to see if
she's just another made-up little doll.'

Some of Nepal's ancient religions had taken strange
turnings. For instance, there were violent and non-
violent Hindus, the former sacrificing any animals
except cows, and Renata would never forget the horror of
walking into a temple shortly after one such sacrifice,
before the blood had been washed away.

Also, Kathmandu had long had its living goddess, a
young girl elected after undergoing hideously terrifying
testing, installed in a temple built around a small square,
from the upper window of which she might look out
when the crowds gathered below, her child's face heavily
made-up.

'I think it's sad,' Renata told Grant. 'Once she reaches
puberty, it's all over, a new goddess is chosen because
she's not deemed pure any longer, and then her life is
virtually over because, I've been told, no Nepalese man
will marry a girl who's been a goddess.'

Grant gave her an amused glance. 'That's a very un-
Western attitude, surely, to regard life as valueless if it
doesn't contain a man.'

'It is, only I don't mean it quite so simplistically; I
don't mean a man is the only aim and be-all and end-all of
a woman's life, but ...' Renata paused, lifting a
shoulder. 'Men and women ... They're two halves of a

whole. I think that's what I mean.'

'We complete each other.' Grant looked at her, his grey eyes compelling. 'When will we be a whole, Renata?'

She caught her breath. 'It's only been a few days, Grant.'

'But we will be?' He was insistent.

Renata looked at him, saw desire kindling in his eyes and felt an answering warmth in her loins.

'Yes,' she whispered. 'Yes, Grant, we will.'

'When?' he asked, still dissatisfied. 'Soon?'

She smiled at his impatience.

'Soon,' she confirmed. 'Not yet, but soon.'

# CHAPTER THREE

GREEN, golden and cosmos-starred, the valley country-side was lyrically beautiful and utterly peaceful, the rice crops looking healthy, but Renata was ill at ease beside Grant in the hired car.

It was Saturday afternoon and they had been to Patan, an outing Renata had enjoyed. She and Grant were getting to know each other, and she knew the time was near when they would become lovers. Since that first night, the only times he touched her were at their partings, kissing her with a hard possessiveness that never failed to leave her gasping and shaken, but sexual tension was never absent between them, and the longer it was denied release, the more intolerable it became. She felt burdened with her need for him, heavy with it, and she knew he must be feeling equally frustrated.

Was she ready for him yet? It was still only a few days since they had met, and there were still areas of reticence, but she was beginning to wonder if they really mattered. She still didn't know what his business in Kathmandu was, or at home for that matter, and she still found herself unable to tell him of the three men she had lost, although she mentioned her mother and Janine quite frequently. She had had opportunities to introduce the subject, as when she had learnt that Grant had been at Cambridge, because her father and brother had both been there, although Darryl had barely scraped through, being more interested in his activities with the Cambridge University Mountaineering Club.

She supposed part of her reluctance to confide in Grant about those things that had affected her deeply was his tendency to want to own her completely. It disturbed her, because she sensed how easily she could surrender to his dominance. He would take her over completely if he knew everything about her and she would lose all her independence of identity. His possessiveness would make him want to obliterate her past, especially that area of it which contained Ang Tsering Lama, and she didn't want that. It was part of her and she didn't want to lose it all, only the grief of her loss.

Additionally, she was just slightly nervous of him perhaps mocking the fact that she had been a Sherpa's sweetheart, and in that she was influenced by her brother. She didn't really believe that Grant was that sort of man; there was nothing petty about him; but she couldn't forget the pain Darryl's attitude had caused her. He had had a curiously old-fashioned attitude towards Sherpas, seeing them still as load-carriers, in stark contrast to their father who had respected Sherpas more than any other people in the world and who had more than once had his life saved by their determined courage and ability to endure.

She had loved her brother and it had hurt to listen to his repeated attempts to talk her out of the relationship, insisting that a Sherpa, any Sherpa, wasn't good enough for her; and she knew that if Grant were to display a similar prejudice, something of her feeling for him would die, unable to survive her disappointment.

She caught herself up critically. No wonder Grant was so possessive and distrustful, when she failed to give him her trust. Of course it wouldn't matter to him that her first love had been a Sherpa; he would merely be jealous of the fact that she had loved someone before him, and she could soothe that in time, she thought. Perhaps she might tell him today . . .

'What are you thinking?' Grant asked suddenly.

Renata's glance was extra-wary. 'You keep asking me that.'

His laugh was abrupt. 'And you keep telling me not to!'

'You can't own my thoughts, Grant,' she pointed out gently.

'Nor share them?'

'Yes, if I want you to, but then I'll tell you what I'm thinking.'

'But I mustn't ask?'

'It's like . . . an invasion of privacy. You've taken over just about every other facet of me, but my thoughts are my own.'

'I am trying, Renata,' he said rather wearily. 'I know you don't like it, that you feel I'm being over-possessive, and I don't really want to force you to share your thoughts with me; I know that I must let you do so in your own good time, when and if you will. That's why I haven't probed about certain areas of your life that you've left blank in talking about yourself and where I sense pain . . . But God, it's hard sometimes when I see that remote look on your face and know you've gone away from me. That's when I want to get inside your head and know everything you're thinking.'

Renata's mouth curved tenderly. In a way, she supposed, his possessiveness would be flattering, reassuring even, if only it didn't seem to threaten her identity.

She was so afraid he would want to take her history away. But she was moved too by his admission of what was probably a form of uncertainty—it was that stark honesty of pride again—and perhaps by sharing all of herself with him and thereby placing her entire trust in him, she would be doing something to increase his trust in her.

She said, 'If you want to know, Grant, my thoughts just then were connected with you.'

He started to ask her a question, stopped himself, glancing at her, and suddenly they were both laughing.

It was going to be all right, Renata though, with a lightening of her spirits. Whatever little problems they had, they could be surmounted as long as they could laugh together, and it was only natural at this early stage that there should be doubts, the occasional touchiness, especially when they had both been knocked off balance by the magnitude and power of the attraction that had flared between them.

'Nevertheless, Renata remained uneasy, for the simple reason that the sky was clearing for the first time in days and she knew that from this part of the country, the Himalaya would be visible, albeit distantly. She supposed she was unduly sensitive, but even the merest glimpse of them affected her badly—and yet she still acknowledged that the great white range was the most beautiful sight she had ever seen in her life, and she had never forgotten her first sight of them as a child, a breathcatching experience. She had seen other ranges, the Karakoram, the Alps, the Hindu Kush, but the Himalaya were matchless, paramount in their austere, icy beauty, their indifference to men and their lives, and she was privileged to have actually been among them and

seen in close-up the graceful spire that was lofty Ama
Dablam, the loveliest peak in the world, and the massive
bulk that was Everest, and cruel Annapurna . . .

But these days she hated to see them and a bad time
was approaching. Three times now she had been
prostrated by the syndrome known to the mind-men as
anniversary grief, and the fourth anniversary was not far
off. She hoped her new absorption with Grant would
lessen it this time, but she couldn't be sure that it would.

Apprehensively, she watched a great rent appear in
the clouds, and then there they were, line upon line of
different white shapes rearing against the blue sky
revealed by the dispersing cloud; but remote and distant,
too far away to oppress her with their cruelty, but a
poignant reminder all the same.

Sadly, she turned her gaze away from the most
stupendous phenomenon in the natural world. The
Himalaya were unconquerable. Not even those men and
the handful of women who strove to stand on the various
summits of those great peaks and succeeded were
conquerors—And they knew that, yet still they climbed,
because they challenged not the mountains but themselves, seeking their personal limits and extending them,
knowing that in those high white places there existed no
mercy for any living creature. That was why they did it,
those whom the mountains owned, loving the game and
the risk better than they loved any fellow creature, and
ultimately the mountains took back most of those whom
they possessed, to keep for ever more, hidden in
crevasses or under seracs.

'You're doing it again,' said Grant in a tight, hard
voice.

'I'm sorry.' Renata's eyes flew to his face as he reduced

speed and pulled over to the side of the road. 'What are you doing?'

'What does it look like?' he retorted, switching off the ignition and turning in his seat to face her. 'You know, Renata, perhaps the reason I keep . . . losing you is that I haven't given you sufficient cause to think about me. Since that night we met, I've refrained from touching you, except for a few unsatisfactory kisses, because you said you needed time. But I'm getting a little tired of it, and especially of the way you seem scarcely to be aware of my presence at times. It's time I made you fully aware of me again.'

'Not here,' Renata protested, unnerved by the glow of almost savage intensity in his eyes.

'Yes, right here,' Grant said inexorably, picking up her hand. 'I've tolerated your reticence long enough. You're a woman of twenty-three, not some shrinking sixteen-year-old who's frightened of the demands of her own body.'

'Grant . . .' she breathed helplessly, the pit of her stomach lurching in violent, pleasurable reaction to the touch of his mouth against her soft palm.

His jaw was slightly rough under her trembling fingertips—he was a two-shave-a-day man—and his lips were parting against her hand, his tongue infinitely erotic in inscribing small moist circles on her palm. A shivering gasp issued from her and instant churning desire assaulted her inwardly so that it required an effort of will to sit still where she was and not attempt to move closer to him.

Grant paused, lowering her hand and laying it flat against his chest, holding it there, and the searing warmth of his body reached her through the thin fabric of his shirt which he wore with casual jeans. Beneath her fingertips she felt the mad race of his heart, matching hers.

'Please . . .' she murmured.

Grant's mouth twisted as he examined her tense face, seeing the wonder and apprehension in her sapphire eyes and the anticipation evidenced by the softening and expectant parting of her lips.

'I've been letting you dictate the pace, and I wonder if you've any idea of the hell it is, wanting you . . . wanting all you have to give, not just tame kisses,' he grated. 'For God's sake, I'm being eaten up by this thing, it's destroying me, and if I don't have you soon . . . I didn't want this, you know, this sort of compulsive obsession, ruling my life, but it's happened, and it would be futile to fight it when we both know that ultimately we'll have to succumb to it and be lovers. Something like this can't be denied.'

'And I never have denied it, Grant,' Renata reminded him huskily, her fingers curling round the material of his shirt as she strove to hang on to sanity. 'I've only asked for time.'

'How much time, damn it?' demanded Grant roughly. 'I can't take much more, Renata. This isn't an ordinary attraction, requiring a decent period of wooing. It was instant and irresistible. How much longer are you going to insist on calling the tune? I warn you, now, I won't endure it much longer . . . And when we do dismantle that barrier you've erected, I'm going to demand full compensation for this time of unnecessary waiting you've put me through.'

'It's necessary to me.'

'I'm probably a fool for considering your wishes at all,' he continued darkly. 'Perhaps I should have ignored your objections that first night and made you mine there and then.'

'And lost me?'

'Would I?'

'I don't know.'

'I was afraid I might,' he admitted candidly. 'That's why, for the first time in my life, I've allowed a woman to call the shots, but I've had just about enough.'

He raised her hand to his mouth again, and Renata moaned, low and soft, as warm, lingering kisses were pressed on her inside wrist and palm, followed by teasing, nibbling kisses all the way up her fingers.

'Grant, please stop,' she choked.

'Why? When we both like it?'

'I'm going crazy,' she protested in a shivering voice, on the very edge of losing control.

'That's the way I want you,' Grant stated arrogantly. 'There are no secrets in your eyes now, Renata. I know everything you're thinking and feeling . . . Or the only thing. You want me.'

He sucked at the sensitive cushioned tips of each of her fingers in turn, teeth gentle, tongue only slightly in motion, until Renata was panting, rigid and trembling as she tried to subdue the humiliatingly swift responses of her body. Her eyes were glazed with desire as sensation spread from her fingers all through her entire being, reaching every tiny nerve-end; shamed colour burned in her cheeks and she whimpered, a tiny helpless sound, as Grant finally took one finger properly into his mouth, tongue sinuously caressing.

'Grant!' She moved jerkily towards him. 'Oh, God, kiss me . . . love me!'

He took her into his arms then, drawing her back

across him so that she was cradled against his chest, but apparently he was in a mood to tease. He showered quick, hot, tormenting little kisses all over her face and jaw and neck, the pulsing hollow at the base of her throat and the warm, satiny skin covering the delicate bones on either side, smiling and denying her satisfaction when she wound her arms about his neck, arching and trying to capture his mouth fully.

'Stop torturing me,' she pleaded throbbingly, her voice just above a whisper.

'Now you know the way I've felt while you've been torturing me all these past days,' he countered mockingly.

But then the smouldering, slumbrous passion she had seen in his eyes awoke fully, exploding into a fire, and his mouth descended on hers, tongue thrusting possessively between her teeth. The fingers of one hand were twined painfully in her hair and the arm supporting her tightened convulsively at her instant, passionate response to this welcome invasion of her mouth.

No car or cart or bicycle passed them on that quiet country road, and the surrounding rice crops were still and serene in the late afternoon sunlight that had broken through, catching the few first tints of autumn in the bordering trees.

Inside the car, heedless of the world outside, Renata and Grant were lost in their own private realm of fierce, compulsive sensuality, utterly absorbed in each other. Clothes were awry as they explored each other, discovering hot flesh that responded to every caress and kiss.

Long sobbing sighs shook Renata, her hot face pressed to Grant's hair-roughened chest between the gaping edges of the shirt she had torn open with frenzied fingers.

She was ablaze with desire, debilitated by it, and he could do as he chose with her—as he was doing, his hands possessing every region of her body which was hot and damp and taut, her tissues swollen with the towering passion of her need. Her pink blouse and bra were open and his hands cupped her engorged breasts, closing over them, and she gasped in ecstasy, her aching nipples throbbing sensitively against his hard fingers.

'Grant!' she groaned in protesting pleasure as he rolled the full, fiery tips between thumbs and fingers, and her body jerked and quivered in response, her blood leaping.

'Oh God, you're beautiful!' he exclaimed hoarsely. 'I want you so badly, Renata . . . I need you!'

It was almost a cry of desperation just before his mouth took hers again and the movements of his hands became feverish, urgent on her breasts, fingers working frantically.

Renata was adrift in swirling, hot darkness, controlled, dictated by the erotic hungering of her body, her womanhood, which seemed to contain a churning, boiling ocean of need; and Grant's was the hard, convulsively shuddering body to satisfy it.

Her white linen skirt had ridden up and was twisted about her upper thighs, and one hand left her breasts to stroke along their taut trembling length, scorching the silken skin. Renata arched, then instinctively shrank from him as he seemed about to go further, pressing her knees together and inadvertently trapping his hand, but Grant was insistent, overcoming her resistance.

A harsh cry broke from her as his hand cupped the soft mound of her femininity, fingers stirring delicately against her warmth, inciting such a rage of wanting as she had never known she was capable of feeling.

She was seared by it, driven to the edge of sanity by the torrent of new sensations that coursed through her now. She could hear a hoarse voice sobbing and pleading, and it was her own.

'Grant . . . please! I want you, I want you . . . Grant!'

The desperation of her entreaty made him glance at her face, and what he saw there cleared the sensual glitter from his eyes.

Renata didn't understand what he did to soothe the ferocious need he had excited. She only knew that at one moment she was on some mindless, multi-sensational plateau, gasping and shuddering; the next she was collapsing weak and limp against him.

He held her until her trembling ceased and she could breathe normally. Then, gently, he moved her back to her side of the car and began to fasten and straighten her clothing as he might have done for a child.

'All right now?' he asked quietly. 'I'm sorry, Renata, I didn't intend things to get so out of control. I don't want our first coming together to be in the cramped confines of a car. Do you understand?'

'Yes, of course,' she sighed lethargically. 'It's all right, Grant. Grant . . .'

There was really nothing to say. Speech seemed too much of an effort. In stark contrast to her tension just a few minutes ago, she felt relaxed to the point of lassitude, with a languorous sense of well-being.

Having buttoned his shirt, Grant sat forward in his seat, his arms resting on the top of the steering-wheel, his face now slightly remote as he stared at the faraway line of white peaks, unseeingly, she thought, but after a minute he looked at her.

'You say you can't see me tonight?' he questioned her.

'Both tonight and tomorrow night there are functions I have to attend at the Embassy,' she confirmed regretfully.

'But you're free tomorrow? I've got a couple of things to see to in the morning, and some paperwork to complete, but I'll pick you up at twelve.'

'What are you planning?' she asked.

'Wait and see,' he replied with a faint smile.

'Grant . . .'

'It's all right, Renata, you still have that time you asked for,' he reassured her. He paused thoughtfully, glancing once more at the distant chain of peaks, seemingly inaccessible from here, and added, 'But not too much. Renata, I want us to be lovers before I have to leave Kathmandu—during this next week, I'm afraid. Then I'll return to you—I'm not sure—in a few weeks, I hope, and we'll have to do some serious talking about the future.'

She smiled. 'The present is quite enough for me to think about at the moment!'

Laughing, he started the car. 'I suppose I'd better be getting you back to Kathmandu if you're on duty this evening.'

'Yes. And Grant . . .' laughter put a lilt in her voice, 'if I don't talk, it's because I'm thinking—about you!'

'That was my intention,' he reminded her amusedly.

She was still thinking about him when he called for her shortly before noon the following day, a second day of rich golden sunshine with only a few clouds in the sky, so the monsoon must be leaving.

Grant was wearing jeans and one of the plain, light-coloured shirts he favoured, and Renata kept her eyes fixed on him as they drove out of Kathmandu, realising anew how virile his appearance was. There was strength in the tanned column of his neck and in his shoulders, evident even when he relaxed. She dropped her gaze to his bare forearms with their covering of fine dark hairs, to his hands, strong but sensitive on the steering-wheel, and finally to his denim-encased thighs, lithely muscled and powerful, and something twisted in her stomach.

She wanted him. What had happened yesterday hadn't been enough; she wanted him fully; and some time in the next few days they would become lovers, and she knew he would be the only lover she would ever have. He didn't need to exercise that possessiveness of his: he owned her completely already, in every way. She was completely and utterly his as, perhaps, he was hers.

She couldn't take her eyes off him while they talked, mostly with her telling him about the innocuous doings at the reception the previous night, and some time later he laughed.

'I love it, Renata—your undivided attention, I mean. You haven't glanced at our surroundings once. Aren't you curious as to where we're going?'

'Never satisfied, are you?' she teased.

'Of course not.'

Obligingly, she took an interest in the country through which they were travelling, recognised the road and stiffened momentarily. She glanced at Grant, then relaxed. He couldn't be expected to know, since she still hadn't brought herself to tell him.

When she could be sure of her voice being steady, she said, 'The foothills, Grant?'

'Yes. Do you like it out there?'

'It's beautiful. I've only been once since I arrived.'

And that hadn't been a happy experience.

'What sort of shoes have you got on? I thought we could walk a bit.'

'My running shoes.' She was wearing jeans and a deep violet T-shirt type top. 'Not that I run, but Karen and I do a lot of walking. But don't forget I have to be back in time for tonight's do at the Embassy.'

She didn't want to go too far into the foothills. As it was, they brought the true Himalaya too close.

They were climbing steeply now, among what might have been called mountains, save for those others beyond, but this was cultivated land, rice crops grown in terraces from top to bottom, every available inch of land put to use.

They had passed through several villages when they came to a place Renata recognised, a wide grassy shelf thrust out over the valley below, and remembering she knew this country better than Grant, she said, 'Stop here for a few minutes, Grant. There should be children to show you . . . a view.'

Looking faintly amused, he obliged. Renata herself averted her eyes from the view as she got out of the car. Almost immediately, the little ones appeared, as if by magic, as not a single small boy had been in sight when they stopped, the scene deserted. They brought small, crude posies of wild flowers, offering them to both adults, and Renata made a fuss of them, returning to the car to get some rupees from her bag to give them, and pretending not to understand them when they tried to make her stand still and look at the view.

But in fairness to a visitor . . . She moved to Grant's side where he stood obediently looking in the direction pointed out by one of the little boys.

'Sagarmatha,' the child was repeating. 'Sagarmatha, Sahib.'

'He means Everest,' Renata interpreted expressionlessly.

Smiling, Grant inclined his head but said nothing, and looked again.

Nervously, Renata took a look. Oh, God, it was so clear today. Quickly she returned her attention to the children, smiling at them but addressing Grant.

'You'll have an even better view if we go higher up.'

He laughed. 'Let's go, then.'

They went on and, knowing he wanted to walk, Renata showed him the best place from which they could begin after parking off the side of the road, which suggestion he accepted without comment.

'Let me know if you get tired,' he said as they set off.

But it was unlikely that she would tire before he, she reflected, since hiking was her main leisure activity here in Nepal and he was a businessman who presumably spent his days in an office when he wasn't flying to the world's commercial capitals, though admittedly he looked like an athlete with nothing in the way of surplus flesh, so perhaps he played squash or attended a gym.

The air was thin up here, and warm, carrying the scent of pines. Wild cosmos grew everywhere, the pink sort and then, the higher they wound, the flame variety, catching the sunlight and somehow imprisoning it, so that the brilliant petals glowed. Higher still, she knew, there would be rhododendron bushes, primulas, and beyond that edelweiss and other alpine plants, and higher still, nothing, no living plant or lichen whatsoever.

She had misjudged Grant, she discovered. He set a rapid pace, apparently unaffected by the thin air after days at the lower altitude of Kathmandu, but perhaps he was conserving his breath, as he was unusually silent. Initially, he waited to help her in difficult places, but, realising she could manage, he went on, and Renata followed at her own pace and by her own route, since it was obvious where he was heading for.

The sun beat down on her head and shoulders as she picked her way upward, always selecting the neatest, most economical line, although Grant seemed to favour the harder way.

All men were alike. An old thought. How many thousands, millions, of women had thought it through the world's ages?

Renata's thoughts wandered here and there, over ideas and hopes and a few memories, but they were hardly deep thoughts as she gave most of her concentration to reaching what would be her only summit, and a puny one beside those beyond.

Grant was waiting for her at the top, but so absorbed in the view that he barely noticed her arrival at first.

After a minute, however, he commented amusedly, 'Looks serene and sunlit enough from here, doesn't it?'

Holding her breath, Renata took a look at the mountain he meant. She wanted to tell him the famous story about Jimmy Roberts on Kalipatar, wondering why the summit climbers were turning back because from where he watched he was unable to see the conditions that forced them down.

But it was fatal to start on climbing stories, so she merely smiled at him before crouching, pretending her shoe lace needed re-tying.

This was ridiculous, she decided a few seconds later. Was she such a coward that she couldn't even look at the thing? Grant was utterly absorbed as anyone had a right to be with the Himalaya in full and glorious view for once; he stood remote and intent, and she knew he had forgotten her.

So why not? Why not attempt an exorcism?

She stood up and let her eyes go in the direction she knew by heart.

No plume, no snow-mist today. They were rarely privileged.

Massive, hulking, the impression was not so much of height as of utter solidity, and yet at 8848 metres, what was higher?

Everest, Sagarmatha, the only black peak in the Himalaya. Chomolongma ... The Tibetan name could mean Goddess Mother of the World or, quaintly, Lady Cow. Ed Hillary was reputed to have called it 'the bastard'.

To Renata it was sexless, too capricious to be male, too impartial to be female. It simply was ...

Tears pricked beneath her eyelids, but she blinked them away, focusing on the mountains again and standing very still, her face a tense mask.

The game, they called it, their pursuit of new routes, harder routes, up higher mountains, until the highest of them all remained, too tempting to be resisted. She had never known a good climber who thought he was challenging a mountain, or conquering it if he achieved the summit. They had all respected the mountains, even feared them. No, generally it was simply the sheer joy of climbing, the need for adventure, the love of risk but not foolish risk, the need to look danger in the face and test both spirit and strength to their utmost limits. Some men claimed to have found their souls by going high; others to have found God.

No, in a sense it wasn't Everest that had taken their men from her mother and herself, but something within the men themselves. Nevertheless, the need to climb it had been greater than their love for their women.

It was a haunted mountain, she supposed. How many, many ghosts walked there for how many women like herself?

Never again, she had sworn. Never again would she mean less to a man than the climbing of a mountain.

But she was ready to let go now, to make her farewells and turn to face her future with this man who stood beside her. She had given enough to the past.

Yet still she looked towards Everest, because somewhere there they lay. Stephen Armstrong. Darryl Armstrong. Ang Tsering Lama.

One by one, Renata let them slip away, until she came to the last. Him she held in her heart a while and silently she offered for him the prayer he had always used:

*O Mane Padme Hum* ...

Then he too was gone, at rest in his own high country, and she turned to the new man.

Grant, it seemed, had had his fill of Everest already, unlike the dead she had just buried, because he was standing looking down at her, watching her calm face.

Free at last, Renata gave him a radiant, unreserved smile and moved towards him, sliding her arms about his waist, and as his arms came round her, she looked up into his dark grey eyes and said, 'I love you, Grant.'

# CHAPTER FOUR

GRANT lifted his mouth from hers, and Renata clung to him dizzily, still shaken by the passion of his kiss.

The grey eyes glowed deeply and he sounded as shaken as she as he said unevenly, 'Ah, God, darling! That's the first time you've ever touched me of your own accord. Renata!'

His mouth covered hers again and a great surge of love and passion rocked her. They held each other so tightly that her breasts, enlarged with the heated blood of intense desire, were crushed against the hard wall of his chest, and hips and thighs were similarly welded together, grindingly, as their erotic, involuntary movements became more and more frenzied as kiss followed long deep kiss.

'I love you, I love you,' Renata whispered against his brown throat when finally her mouth was free, her fingers stroking the back of his neck.

Grant shuddered, moving his hands up and down the length of her back, caressing her spine, making her gasp at the exquisite sensations he induced.

'Hearing you say it makes me even more impatient for you,' he murmured urgently against her smooth, scented hair. 'Darling, do you have to go to this thing at the Embassy tonight? Can't we . . . be together?'

'I must,' she said regretfully. 'I have duties to perform and we won't finish until very late. But tomorrow night, Grant . . . Can I cook dinner for you? And I'll tell you my life story if you like, and then . . . and then——'

'Yes, and then!' Grant laughed shakily. 'All right. And I shall have things to tell you too, my darling.'

That he loved her, she thought, resting her head on his shoulder and wondering why he couldn't tell her now, but perhaps he wanted to wait until they made love.

Sensing that he was restraining himself and realising that he didn't want to let the situation get out of control as it had yesterday, she was glad. To make love here in view of her old enemy would be inappropriate, and Renata disengaged herself.

'Should we be going?' she asked, and Grant nodded, smiling in acknowledgement of her understanding.

Turning to descend, she threw a last glance at the Himalaya, but neither in defiance nor in triumph. Her eyes revered their beauty, but she looked too now in acceptance of what they had done to her, because she had survived, and she had a man who was free of their fatal fascination. It was a peacemaking of sorts, but they stood as they always had, icily indifferent to all humankind, to lives and hopes and dreams. Mentally, she shrugged. They were too much for her, beyond the reach of any philosophy she possessed.

Then she turned and followed Grant.

It was a happy afternoon. He waited for her on the descent, and they held hands over the easy parts.

Down at last, Grant said, 'I'm starving! I've had no lunch, have you?'

'No. There's a sort of lodge not far from here where we can get something to eat and drink. We could walk down and come back for the car afterwards,' Renata added.

'If you're not too tired?'

'No. Are you?'

He smiled, shaking his head, so they walked on, arms about each other now that they were on comparatively level ground, following an easily defined track, and still the sun shone, catching the colours of wild flowers and fluttering butterflies. Once they passed a trio of small shepherd boys sprawled on a grassy ledge, enjoying the warmth, and Renata was glad to see it, knowing what a hard life these people had when winter came. The children greeted them shyly, quieter and less importunate than the children in the valley towns.

They sat outside at the lodge, the investment of a local man who had prospered as a guide, in a high place with the rearing Himalaya once more in view, the sunlight making them a dazzlingly white backdrop to the steep brown and green hills above which they sat, but Renata no longer needed to avert her eyes. She didn't stare at them either, though, as most visitors were apt to do, hypnotised by their mighty magnificence, not quite able to believe they were actually seeing them; she preferred the closer things, which seemed to have more reality now, like the blaze of a patch of flame cosmos nearby, beautiful but gently incapable of overwhelming. The mountains had become dreamlike, part of her past, with no relevance in her life any longer.

But most of all, she looked at Grant, her man and her love, soon to be her lover. She believed he loved her too, although he hadn't yet spoken the words; she hoped he did, because she knew now beyond all doubt that he was the only man she would ever love. She wanted to share all her life with him, be his wife if that was what he wanted, and have his child.

These were rare hours of pure, conscious happiness, her old love at last laid to rest and the new beside her as she ate one of her favourite meals, a simple one of yak cheese on brown bread, garnished with cherries and walnuts. The joy endured too as they strolled back up to the car later, talking desultorily and touching all the while, the urgency of their need still there but kept under control now that they knew the waiting was nearly over.

'Tomorrow night,' said Grant when he dropped her at her flat, and the words were more a promise than a question.

'Yes,' Renata breathed rapturously as his mouth touched the corner of hers. 'Oh, Grant, it's been such a perfect day!'

'Our nights together will be even more perfect,' he retorted, eyes glinting, and she shivered as they wrapped their arms about each other for a last kiss—and another, and another . . .

There wasn't much time left in which to ready herself for tonight's affair at the Embassy, a glamorous, glittery occasion in contrast to the serious tone of last night's function, but her delirious happiness contributed a buoyant energy which caused her to sail through the ritual of bathing, dressing and making up.

It was after two in the morning when she finally got to bed, but with this new feeling of wellbeing stemming from her happy anticipation she seemed to need scarcely any sleep, and she was up earlier than usual, singing quietly in the shower while she tried to decide what to cook for Grant that night, Western cuisine or one of the Nepalese meals she had learnt to cook as a child when the whole family had lived in Nepal for a couple of years.

Renata would never forget that Monday, for a variety of reasons. She carried her excitement with her to the Embassy, wondering if Grant would ring her during the day, planning the ingredients she would purchase either at lunchtime or after work, deciding what to wear . . .

She found it difficult to concentrate on her work, but fortunately it was mostly routine today, for all of them. People wandered in to chat and she listened with half her mind, dreaming of Grant, recalling the perfection and promise of their hours together the previous afternoon.

Nothing could hurt her now. She heard with complete equanimity the reminder that there was another small party scheduled for Tuesday night as a courtesy to the British expedition to Everest to be held, not at the Embassy, but at a colleague's home. She knew she would be expected to look in for a while, but the prospect no longer troubled her. She had no connection with that world now, and nothing to lose to it.

Manning the desk of the colleague who had some responsibility for assisting the expedition while they were still in Kathmandu when he was called away briefly, she could even glance over his lists in idle curiosity and with an absence of the old horror, interested to see at the bottom of the list the name of Bill Thurlow, from one of the major London dailies. He had accompanied several expeditions to Everest and had even gone up through the Ice Fall on a few occasions. She caught sight of the ubiquitous 'Ang' and was glad to see that those Sherpas who were joining the expedition here in Kathmandu, where many of them now chose to live, were also invited to the party, and she wondered if there were any she knew. Mingma, the Sirdar or head Sherpa, could be the Mingma she knew. Ang Phurba? She remembered an Ang Phurba, remote and ascetic, but this could be another one, and of course she knew Harish Gupta, the Nepalese liaison officer.

It must be quite a small expedition. They usually were these days, with just a handful of Sherpas instead of the great numbers who had accompanied the old siege-style expeditions. It was all much more democratic now, but there had to be an official leader in order to satisfy the requirements of the Nepalese government who laid down strict regulations regarding the climbing of their mountains.

Renata's eyes travelled to the top of the list.

There it was.

Grant Fowler.

She wondered if this was how it felt falling off a mountain, plummeting from the heights to an icy, agonising death far below.

'No!' she moaned, bent over the desk, the pain of it physical, tearing at her insides, rending her.

Her colleague's phone rang and she stared at it blankly for long moments before lifting the receiver and muttering an explanation of his absence in a dull, lifeless voice. The receiver clattered as she replaced it and she sat staring at the desk, thinking she was going to be sick but quite unable to move.

He had lied to her . . .

'Grant,' she whispered, wishing for numbness, but there was only anguish.

He was going to Everest and she would lose him too, whom she could least bear to lose.

Never again, she had vowed, and now it was too late. She loved him, and that mysterious enemy existed in him too, the need to climb.

Too late, because he had lied to her, or withheld the truth anyway. A lie by omission, but undoubtedly deliberate.

Why?

Pain in the palms of her hands made her uncurl her clenched fists and she stared at the little bleeding crescents her nails had made.

'Please, no!' She spoke aloud, a desperate entreaty, and she was praying that it be made untrue. But there it was in black and white. Expedition Leader: Grant Fowler. 'No!'

It had become a threnody of pain, and she sat there in her colleague's chair, arms wrapped about her own body now in an instinctive attempt to stop the chill shuddering horror that gripped her, and rocking back and forth in her grief, as if he were dead already.

A few thoughts began to mingle with what had been an entirely emotional reaction up until now. No wonder he had seemed amused at moments yesterday, notably when she had told him the children meant Everest when they had pointed it out, calling it Sagarmatha. He would have known that; he would know its shape with no help from them. It had probably been his personal lodestar for long years.

He had lied!

A cold anger was gathering in her now. She picked up the main list and read swiftly through all the names. She knew none of the other climbers either, Jones, Anderson and Fiore, but that wasn't surprising when for the last four years she had deliberately ignored everything to do with mountaineering. They would be the new men who had come up to replace those who had gone. The expedition doctor, Leo Summers, she did know, however; he had come to her parents' home for a meeting with her father just before he had set out on his last fatal trip seven years previously and been signed on as the doctor to that fateful expedition.

She read the climbers' names again. Fowler, Jones, Anderson and Fiore. Detachedly, her old knowledge of the game surfacing, she realised they must be good, in the first place, to have gained permission for Everest from the Nepalese government and secondly because, as she had heard earlier, the expedition had the full support of the Mount Everest Foundation at home, plus generous sponsorship from some reliable bodies, including Bill Thurlow's paper.

Renata knew too much to be reassured or comforted. Her father had been good, the best. So had the other two, young as they had been.

Her colleague returned, staring at her white shocked face and asking if she felt unwell, and Renata gave him back his desk with a murmured denial of illness, her voice flat and dead. She didn't return to her own office immediately. She knew there were books on mountaineering in the Embassy, kept almost as reference books, inevitable in a place like Nepal, and she found the one she required, a Who's Who of mountaineering.

At her desk, grateful that she was alone, she looked up Grant Fowler, her icy anger growing, mingling with the agony and despair of her heartbreak.

His was the traditional climbing background. Public school, Cambridge, the Cambridge University Mountaineering Club. He had told her some truths. He did have various business interests, some impressive, and in his early climbing years he had personally financed his own expeditions. His career record told her she would have heard of him in the last few years and might actually have done so before that, but everything to do with mountaineering, every small memory, had been deliberately buried, blanked out, by the self-induced amnesia which had gradually become an ingrained habit.

Was there anything he hadn't climbed? From the Central Pillar of Frêney on Mont Blanc and the other great European mountains as a very young man, Yosemite, the world's finest rock wall, and a spectacular ascent of the nose of El Capitan, Aconcagua, the tallest mountain in the Western hemisphere, Cerro Torre, perhaps the most difficult in the world, and Mount McKinley; to pioneering a brilliant new route up Mount Kenya's Diamond Couloir, one of the world's most challenging difficult ice climbs. Trango's nameless tower had followed, and other climbs in the Pamirs and the Hindu Kush. Then the eight-thousanders, thirteen of the world's fourteen being in the Himalaya or the Kara-koram. Annapurna twice, by the original Herzog route and by the South Face, Dhaulagiri, Nanga Parbat, and on to Kangchenjunga, the world's third highest moun-tain on the border of Nepal and Sikkim where climbers stopped a few feet short of the actual summit in deference to the belief of the Sikkimese people that it was sacred.

Only Everest was left. Grant had been injured on K2, the second highest mountain in the world, four years ago, but had attempted it again, successfully, two years later.

Still white-faced, her mouth twisted, Renata closed the book and returned it, uninterested in the histories of the other team members.

Why hadn't he told her?

A struggle was beginning deep inside her, a desperate fight to avoid the pain that was inevitable when she lost Grant. She wanted not to be in love with him; she wanted to hate him; frantically she tried to convince herself that the discovery of his lie had killed her love, but the pain was with her already, inescapable and devastating, as if she had lost him to the mountain already.

She loved him, she hated him. Emotionally, Renata writhed in tormented protest against the knowledge that it had happened to her again. Once again, she loved a man possessed of that mysterious compulsion to climb. He might love her too, but a man's love for a woman could never measure up to that other restless, questing obsession that made widows of women. He would always go back to the mountains, again and again.

Perhaps there was something wrong with her too, though, she reflected with a flash of angry humour, a compulsion of another sort. What was wrong with her, that the only men she seemed able to fall in love with were those who needed to go high? Why couldn't she have fallen in love with, say, a stockbroker or a teacher, or any man just as long as his most dangerous obsession was something along the lines of gardening or building model cars?

People at the Embassy started noticing her white, stricken face, the sick shock in her eyes, and in the early afternoon she was ordered home in one of the Embassy cars, but she persuaded the driver to drop her at a spot from which she could walk into the old part of Kathmandu.

She hardly knew why she wanted to do so, except that alone in her flat she suspected that grief would overwhelm her utterly. She crossed a wide intersection in a daze, and only the quick reactions of a cyclist prevented her being sent flying. She felt sick, tortured by the unbearable truth as she wandered down a road and came

at last to the dark narrow streets and alleys of the old
town.

Her walking was aimless, and she noticed nothing
about her, desolate with a sense of loss. Nothing was left.
All the bright happy dreams with which she had awoken
that morning were gone, annihilated by a name on a
piece of paper and the realisation of a terrible truth.

She pictured Grant, his vitality and strength, and then
she saw him falling endlessly from a high place and lying
broken somewhere below, beyond recognition, and it
was no over-vivid imagination that drew these pictures
but an all too realistic awareness of the facts. She knew
too much to have any illusions, brought up among men
who took the risks Grant took, encouraged from an early
age to be interested in the game. She knew the odds.

She couldn't go through it again, she thought feverishly. She just could not face it another time ... She
would not.

From the roof-top to which he often climbed in order
to observe the comings and goings in his part of the city,
five-year-old Hamir spotted her, a slender figure in a soft
grey wool dress with three-quarter-length sleeves and
sheer matching tights. He saw her white, vulnerable face
grow set and hard, and went leaping down the outside
staircase, darting after her and tugging at her skirt until
she noticed him.

'Sick?' he demanded when she paused, looking down
at him.

'No. No, not sick, Hamir,' she answered seriously,
wishing she could reassure him with a smile, but her
mouth wouldn't make the right movements.

'Sad?' he enquired interestedly then, his brown eyes
concerned and friendly as he gazed up into her own with

their look of stunned suffering.

'Yes, sad,' Renata agreed huskily.

'Man gone?' he guessed.

'Not yet, but he is going,' she told him, the first person she had been able to talk to about it since she had discovered the truth.

'England?'

'No. He's a mountaineer, Hamir, a climber,' she explained. 'He's going to Sagarmatha.'

Hamir was no Sherpa. He looked grave, shaking his head. 'Bad,' he offered.

'Very bad.'

He thought a moment. 'Maybe success,' he ventured to encourage her, but even he sounded doubtful.

Success would be to get off the mountain alive, she reflected bleakly, but there would always be other mountains.

She couldn't face it again, she thought emphatically for the second time, her mouth tightening as she moved on, Hamir wandering along at her side perhaps in the belief that she needed company.

She couldn't go through the waiting and the terror for a start. Stephen Armstrong had raised his children to respect the mountains, but although she had learned during childhood of the deaths of other climbers, friends of her father's who had visited their home, Renata had not learnt to fear them until Stephen's own death. Fear had gripped her whenever Darryl was on a mountain after that, and had made the waiting hell that last time when another's safety had become even more important than Darryl's. The bitterness and resentment had come only after that second, double loss, when she had been forced to accept what had felt like a betrayal, the fact that mountains or the climbing of them meant more to men than their women.

Never again! She tried to snatch the old resolve back, to hug it to her, but it was too late. She loved and she would lose again. She had lost already.

Hamir kept pace with her until they passed an old friend, a shopkeeper who seemed to sell nothing but Waltzing Matilda hats. Then he darted off, after asking anxiously, 'See you?'

'Yes, of course,' she assured him, trying to smile over further painful realisation.

It had been a mistake to accept this posting to Nepal. It could never have happened anywhere else. Dear God, if only she could have been sent somewhere absolutely flat, to some completely hill-less country, she would never have met Grant Fowler.

Somehow, she found herself back at her flat, and somehow the afternoon had slipped away, the passing of time unnoticed in her misery. She had dumped her bag and kicked off her shoes, but no more. She sat huddled on the couch with its soft covering of pashmina shawls, her despair beyond tears, beyond any cathartic act of violence. She could only sit and suffer.

Not until the last light of day had failed did she stir, getting up and drawing the curtains, switching on lights throughout the flat.

When the doorbell buzzed she knew it was Grant. The security man in the lobby, accustomed to seeing him with Renata by now, would have let him through, and he had said he would come as soon as his business allowed.

She knew what his business in Kathmandu was now, she reflected bitterly, standing in the hall and staring at the door. She knew so well the endless dealings with

Customs all expeditions had, the paperwork and permits that had to be in order, the sorting of stores and equipment, the clothing, climbing gear and sleeping-bags which the regulations required the Sherpas to be provided with, the frantic last-minute purchasing of extra food, the hundred other arrangements to be dealt with, the last-minute alarms about the adequacy of tentage and ropes, the consignments of crampons, jumars, dead-men and other items that mysteriously went missing in the pre-expedition chaos . . .

Oh, she knew now.

She had neglected to put the security chain on, so she opened the door wide, and a sudden fit of violent shivering gripped her as she stood looking wordlessly at Grant who wore pale stone-coloured pants and an open-necked shirt.

'Renata.' Grant moved as if to take her in his arms, then stopped, noticing her pallor and the feverish over-brightness of her eyes.

'Go away.' The words emerged in a low tone ending on a gasp.

'You're sick,' he guessed concernedly. 'Renata, let me——'

'You lied to me!'

He was instantly alert, staring at her assessingly with narrowed eyes, his face suddenly hard.

'What is this?' he asked quietly.

'You lied,' she repeated dully. 'You're a climber . . . the leader of the present British expedition to Everest.'

He relaxed slightly at that. 'I've been surprised you hadn't found out before now, working at the Embassy.'

Renata looked at him in disbelief. 'Get out,' she said, afraid the sudden welling resentment in her breast would swamp what little self-control she possessed.

Grant's eyes grew stormy. 'Don't you think you're overreacting a bit? No, I damned well won't get out!'

In fact, he had moved into the hall, shutting the door with a sharp click before taking her by the arm and moving her into the lounge, ignoring the way she flinched and tried to pull away from him.

'Please, Grant! It's impossible, it was a mistake . . . I can't — Oh, God, why didn't you tell me?' she concluded accusingly, almost weeping as she finally wrenched her arm from his grasp.

'I wish I had, as it seems to have upset you so much. All right, I suppose I did lie, by omission, and I'm sorry,' he said heavily. 'But it wasn't with any . . . underhand intention, Renata, and it started for the simplest and silliest of reasons. Will you listen, and then perhaps you'll understand? I'm not exactly a Messner, but even so, for years now, ever since I've been a name in mountaineering, there have been some women—not all—who've come on really strong, as soon as they've realised who I am, trying to get into my bed by fair means or foul——'

'This time you hit on one who'd have run a million miles the minute she realised who and what you were,' Renata cut in harshly.

'Let me finish! I'm not a sex maniac, I don't need hordes of women who are more interested in my public status than in me, and I get bloody tired of it at times. I was even getting to the stage where I was becoming paranoically suspicious of every woman who seemed attracted to me, wondering if it was me or just my name and fame she was really interested in.' He paused and a faint smile touched his mouth. 'When I met you, it was so refreshing. You obviously hadn't a clue who I was, and so

I decided to keep it that way for a while, always wondering when you'd hear something at the Embassy, and somehow I never got round to telling you . . . We had other things to talk about, didn't we? But it was one of the things I was going to tell you tonight. If my . . . small deceit has upset you, then I'm sorry.'

Renata was silent, conscious of a very tiny area of relief because it had occurred to her, just as he began his explanation, that he might have known who she was and her history, and kept quiet about his mountaineering in the knowledge that she would find it unacceptable. Obviously, however, he had never connected her with Stephen Armstrong, and her relief stemmed from the knowledge that Grant's editing of the truth didn't arise out of such cruel cynicism.

'Renata?' Grant said questioningly, moving towards her, but she backed away from him.

'No! Grant, it's not the lie, or. . . or rather, the lateness of the truth,' she qualified fairly. 'Don't you see? It's the fact! I can't . . . I can't have a . . . a relationship with you, I can't have a climber in my life.'

'Why not? What difference does it make?' Grant demanded tautly, and Renata sensed his growing impatience. 'So I climb; so what? I'm still the same person.'

'No! Just go away, Grant, please . . . Please!' she repeated urgently. 'I don't want you in my life.'

'You've already got me in your life,' he countered brutally, his eyes growing stormier by the second. 'For God's sake, Renata, you're being stupid over this. I can't see what your objection is——'

'No, of course not!' she concurred scathingly, all the

old bitterness welling up, even more intense and stinging than before.

'I've already warned you that I would have to go away for a while, even if I omitted to tell you why, but this was another thing I wanted to discuss with you tonight,' he went on. 'When I return——'

Renata's hysterical little laugh cut him short. 'When you return! How do you know you will, Grant?'

She had never said it to any other climber before, and she experienced a moment of guilt, knowing the magnitude of the solecism.

'Don't be a fool, Renata——'

'Who's the fool? Isn't climbing a difficult and dangerous pursuit, Grant?' she demanded savagely, breaking more rules as the acid-sharpness of her resentment gathered in strength.

'Of course there's an element of risk,' he admitted angrily.

'And that's why I can't have a relationship with you. I will not,' she stated so intensely it was a renewal of her old vow. 'I won't commit myself to a man who . . . who's prepared to throw his life away in attempting to climb a mountain.'

'I'd be throwing my life away if I didn't climb,' Grant responded arrogantly.

They all felt like that, she recalled bleakly.

'What comes after Everest, Grant?' she asked sardonically. 'What mountain, I mean?'

Momentarily distracted, he said, 'We've got permission for a winter season attempt on Lhotse, always assuming we're sufficiently fit after Everest. Renata, what——'

She was laughing, amazed to find she could, but his

reaction had been so typical of the climbing men she had known, and incredibly she felt almost nostalgic. It was one of those mad moments which made her wonder about herself, regarding Grant with tender indulgence just because he was so very much a mountain man.

But she recovered swiftly, shocked at herself, angry with him.

'That's it, then. I'm not too sure what I'm supposed to say, Grant. It's been nice knowing you? Goodbye, one way or another, anyway.'

Rage flashed in Grant's grey eyes, but he controlled it, surveying her in silence for a few seconds.

Finally he said, 'Are you sure all this sudden temperament isn't manufactured, something you've contrived because you've developed cold feet since yesterday's commitment and are looking for an excuse to extricate yourself? Is that it, Renata?'

'No, you don't understand. I was committed, until I found out——'

'You're still committed.'

'No! I'm not, I can't be——'

His smile was taunting. 'You love me, remember?'

Renata flinched at his mockery. 'That's why I want you out of my life now, while it's still early enough, perhaps, for me to stop loving you.'

Grant's face had darkened and a possessive light burned in his eyes as he took a step towards her.

'Oh no, Renata,' he told her harshly, 'I won't let you do that. You made a commitment and I'm not letting you back out of it for whatever insane reason you've dreamed up.'

'Grant——'

His hands were on her shoulders, his fingers biting into

her flesh through the soft material of her dress.

'You're mine.' The words were as primitive as the expression in his eyes. 'You belong to me, we belong together, and I'll prove it to you, now.'

# CHAPTER FIVE

'GRANT, you don't understand,' Renata was gasping, trapped and held fast against his hard body by the steeliness of the arms bound across her back, arms with a mountaineer's strength.

'Oh, but I do,' Grant returned sardonically, his face very close to hers. 'I gave you too much time, you got scared and now you think you want out. But I won't let you . . . I've waited for you long enough. You know this is inevitable, it's something we promised each other the first time we looked at each other, before we'd even spoken a word. You know it's true, don't you?'

'Grant, please, let me explain,' Renata beseeched desperately, struggling to free herself, but she knew her frantic movements against his body were only serving to excite him.

'You're mine,' he reiterated, his lips hot against her cheek. 'God, Renata, you're cold . . . But you'll be warm soon, I promise you.'

Already warmth was stealing through her veins as his mouth covered hers. A melting weakness invaded her body and limbs; she felt boneless, faint with the sensations his kiss induced, and she knew her body would betray her if she didn't stop him now.

'Please, Grant, don't do this,' she implored when he lifted his head.

'I must,' he claimed tempestuously. 'We both knew

this was going to happen tonight. You haven't cooked that meal that was going to precede it, have you, and I don't think either of us is in the mood to eat out. We can do our talking afterwards. Right now, all I want is to make love to you, to show you you're mine and put an end to this sudden resistance of yours.'

'I can't . . . I don't want . . . Please don't!' Renata knew her voice was beginning to lack conviction.

'You want, Renata,' he contradicted her arrogantly. 'You want, the same way I do, and after tonight you'll realise the futility of these protests and the stupidity of our having denied ourselves all this past week. We belong together.'

He was kissing her again, and as she had anticipated, her body was betraying her. She hated what he was, but the discovery of it had done nothing to diminish her love and her desire for him. She was responding to him mindlessly, all thought sliding away under the erotic onslaught of his mouth, and even her anguish, resentment and fear were pale, faint emotions as her love for him welled up, filling all her being.

Her hands began to move on him, plucking feverishly at his shirt, caressing his shoulders, the back of his neck, trembling fingers threading their way into his dark hair. Grant's hands too were straying over her, stroking down the length of her back, grasping her waist and hips, discovering the shape of her buttocks and upper thighs, lifting her up close against him.

Renata moaned faintly, half in protest, but also with desire, and involuntarily her hips began to stir against him, jerkily at first before finding the age-old rhythm, the circular motion that symbolised the act of love. She felt Grant shudder against her, and a draught down the length of her back meant he had found the zip of her dress.

He stepped back a little, easing the soft fabric from her shoulders, and the garment slipped down around her body and fell to the floor. For a moment he stood looking at her, at the swell of her breasts emerging from her snowy bra, at the soft curve of her slim hips and the flatness of her stomach, and at the graceful, vulnerable slope of her shoulders. His face was a tight dark mask, but his eyes were almost black with stormy passion as a harsh sigh escaped him and he picked her up in his arms.

'Where's your bedroom?' he demanded urgently.

Renata couldn't answer him, but he found it anyway, carrying her as easily as if she were a baby, and the cold little thought intruded again—the strength of the mountaineer, accustomed to moving upward in dangerously thin air, a rucksack weighing anything up to fifty pounds on his back.

The reminder of what he was brought a moment of sanity, and Renata tried to roll away from him as he deposited her on her bed, which was covered with a duvet, but Grant fell on her, his mouth claiming hers again, and she was trapped beneath him, her will to resist waning as their joined mouths became a fiery vortex.

'Grant, I can't . . . please!' she tried again, but he was deaf to her protests, a brilliant, reckless light in his eyes as he stripped her of her remaining garments.

Then his mouth was at hers, and at her jaw and throat and shoulders, and one hand was stroking her filling breasts, possessively, seductively. Renata's loins exploded into molten, clamorous life, vibrant with need. Her breasts were swollen, and aching, the nipples throbbing under the stimulation of his fingers, and her resentment faded again as she panted, tearing at his shirt, and all that mattered in the world was that she feel his body on hers, without any barrier between them.

'God, I want you,' he groaned, having shrugged out of his shirt, and she gasped as he bent to her, feeling his mouth at her breasts, the slight roughness of his jaw rasping the tender ivory flesh.

His mouth was hot and hard, claiming her, making her his, and her hands clutched at his shoulders while her head moved violently from side to side on the pillows. She was helpless with desire, melting for him, and when he sat up to remove the rest of his clothes she tried to help him, her hands urgent and impatient.

Then they were naked in each other's arms, only able to breathe in long shuddering sighs as desire mounted. Mouths and hands were wildly out of control, and now Renata was as possessive as Grant, uninhibitedly exploring his hard body, revelling in the torrid heat of his flesh, the hardness of his thighs and his flat stomach, stroking the dark body hair with loving fingertips, discovering the male shape of him and hearing his hard groan of barely controlled desire as she felt its physical evidence leaping and quivering against her hand.

It was her first full knowledge of a man's body, and her hands and mouth touched him with a wonder and adoration that were almost reverent, awed by the way she could make him sigh and groan until with a sudden violent movement he pushed her back against the pillows again.

His mouth covered hers, while one hand moved compulsively down over her pulsing body, sliding over the sweat-dampened flesh to cross her flat stomach and the dark triangle between her thighs, coming at last to where she craved him. A moist heat throbbed beneath his fingers; she felt full and heavy with desire, crying out as he exerted delicate pressure, her slender thighs shaking with the utterly female need to hold him. His lips followed the downward journey of his hands, and Renata was weeping with intolerable need by now, her body jerking spasmodically when she felt him take her into his mouth, so intimately that hot colour flooded her face.

'Grant . . .' She clung to him as he moved up over her, opening her wet eyes to look up into his taut, dark face, so unbearably beloved. 'Oh God, Grant, why did you have to be a mountaineer?'

His mouth twisted in sudden impatient anger. 'Don't think about it now. We'll talk afterwards.'

Renata felt the hardness of him between her legs, his hair-roughened thighs rasping the smooth skin of hers as his hands grasped her hips, lifting her, making her submit.

She looked up into his face as she felt him move against her moistness, and it was taut and drawn, his eyes glazed with desire.

Grant conquered her instinctive rigidity and Renata gasped, briefly fighting the intrusion, subjected for the first time in her life to a man's driving, dominating passion. He had drawn back and thrust deeper before becoming aware of her reaction, and already the pain was dulling and in its place came a throbbing pleasure as her warm, moist femininity began to welcome his rigid and penetrant maleness.

Now she sensed that he strove to control the pace, the slow, uneven strokes of his possession an indication of the difficulty with which he did so, his face tight with strain, his mouth twisted in anguish.

Love for him suddenly flooded Renata as she saw his agony, and she clung to him as she began to move with him, finding his rhythm. She heard the strange soft cries she was making as pleasure grew more intense, becoming rapture, and heard too the harsh strangled sound he made as her response banished the last of his control. His thrusting became faster, deeper, and Renata's nails dug into his shoulders. She rocked and swayed with the force of their united movement, still crying her pleasure, and he held her, mastering her, so undeniably his.

Ecstasy mounted and she pulsed against his hardness, holding and releasing as he rode her with love, ceaselessly, and sharp sounds of pleasure were torn from him too. This was true possession, the impelling drive of his body in hers, back and forth and deeper and deeper, and in her surrender she received in return an ecstasy undreamt of, so exquisite that she was fainting with it, her head thrown back, her face contorted.

They seemed to explode together in a wild, frenzied crescendo of sensation that held every part of her body, convulsing her as she was suspended, arched rigid and shaking in a final rigour of ecstasy, gasping and sobbing hoarsely in his arms, as he shuddered against her in his own tumultuous release.

It was a while before the hot, voluptuous darkness cleared from Renata's mind. When it did, she opened her eyes and looked down at their two sprawling, collapsed bodies, still glistening with their mingled sweat, Grant's so dark and infinitely masculine, hers ivory-pale, marked here and there with the evidence of their turbulent lovemaking.

With a sort of detached curiosity, she raised her eyes to Grant's face and saw that he too was looking at what he had done to her. Then, sensing her regard, he looked at her face, his eyes darkly grey and unfathomable, half screened by dark eyelashes.

'I was never sure if you were a virgin or not,' he admitted reluctantly. 'I thought you might just possibly be, but then, when the moment came, I wanted you so badly that I forgot. I'm sorry.'

Renata turned her head away without answering him. Anguish was renewing itself and she couldn't speak.

'Renata?' he said, gently questioning, after a few moments.

'Get out,' she said flatly, still not looking at him.

'Oh, for God's sake,' he sighed on a note of weary exasperation. 'Renata, I know I rushed you, that I was unsympathetic, considering your lack of experience, but . . . Oh, hell, I had to make love to you before I leave Kathmandu . . . I don't really know why. To make sure of you, to have something to both remember and look forward to while I'm away . . . But most of all, simply because I wanted you so much. When I return——'

'If you return,' she corrected, still in that dead, dull tone. 'Then don't come near me. You wouldn't listen, would you? I said I didn't want you in my life, and I didn't want to make love, but you didn't listen. You just went ahead, believing that what you wanted was more important than my wishes . . . Oh, what's the use? Just go away, Grant. Leave me alone.'

'Is all this still to do with the fact that I'm going to Everest?' he demanded tautly, and she felt him sit up. 'Renata, listen to me. Let me explain about climbing. Of course there's an element of risk, but it's exactly that which engenders an extra degree of alertness. That's what climbing is all about. It's not about standing on a summit. We're none of us suicidal types, we love life and we're all geared to surviving——'

'Forget it, Grant,' she said, looking at him at last, her eyes bitter. She had heard it all before, and none of them could ever really explain why they did it. 'I don't want to hear. You wouldn't listen to me, and now I'm not listening to you.'

'I'm listening now,' he snapped, eyes beginning to blaze.

'All right, then listen to this,' she said in a quiet, dry little voice. 'I hate you, Grant, and I want you out of my flat and out of my life.'

His fingers came round her wrist, tightening with a fierce cruelty. 'Say that again,' he commanded. 'Tell me you hate me and look at me while you're saying it.'

She was looking at him, and her sapphire eyes were dead as she did so, with no spark in their depths, because she was looking at his death on the mountain and at the knowledge that there would never be joy in her life again because she had loved him and would never love anyone else.

'I hate you,' she repeated lifelessly.

Grant looked at her for a few seconds. Then he released her wrist. There was no amusement in his abrupt laugh.

'Yesterday you loved me, tonight you hate me,' he taunted. 'What happened?'

'The love died.'

'You mean I killed it, don't you?' he challenged sharply on a note of intense anger. 'No, Renata, what I did was . . . I made love to you. I know I hurt you, but afterwards . . . I know what happened afterwards. It's not something to regret. It will always be that way between us, you know that, and now you're attempting to deny——'

'You still haven't understood, it's not that . . .' She stopped, realising she had begun to shiver violently, and she sat up, shifting until she could pull out the edge of the duvet and wriggle under it. 'Please, Grant, I've had enough. Just go!'

He looked at her in angry silence for a moment, his gaze stormy and rebellious, and she looked back at him tiredly, unable to say more. Then, slowly, he stood up and gathered his clothes before going into her bathroom.

When she could hear the shower, Renata slipped out from under the duvet and went to the wardrobe, extracting her full-length robe, a silk and cotton mixture in a rich shade of cream with palest apricot revers, cuffs and tie-belt.

She had donned it and was gathering up the garments Grant had stripped from her earlier, the pale grey tights going into the tiny bin under the dressing-table, when he emerged from the bathroom, dressed now and still looking furious.

'Obviously you're not in a state to listen to any reason tonight, so I may as well go, but I haven't done with you yet, Renata,' he warned on a note of controlled savagery. 'I've got a hundred things to do before we leave on Wednesday, but I'll see you when we get back. Or if you see sense for yourself you could come out to Thyangboche and wait for us there when we're due off the mountain.'

Renata shuddered at the memories the name evoked and shook her head.

'It's no use, Grant,' she said quietly.

'I won't accept that what was between us is suddenly dead,' he asserted harshly. 'It's not dead for me, I still want you, more than ever now, and I don't believe it's dead for you either. You're mine, Renata, you belong to me.'

She made a small, distressed gesture of denial. Those possessive words, which had once unnerved her, had become familiar and she had grown to believe that they were true, but no longer. She would never belong to a mountaineer.

Grant stood looking at her for a while, and she felt too drained to say anything, simply waiting for him to go.

'You're mine, Renata. Don't forget it,' he offered again eventually. 'I'll be seeing you.'

'No.'

'Yes.' He paused, on the point of leaving the bedroom. 'You'll be all right?'

'Yes.'

'Oh God, Renata, this is ridiculous!' he exploded. 'Let me stay with you tonight. We belong together, and I've only got one more night in Kathmandu. Darling——'

'No!' Renata's voice cracked. Somehow his sudden emotional outburst had stirred her, and the idea of spending the rest of the night in his arms seemed the most desirable thing in the world—except that it would bind her to him all the more securely, and already she was unsure if she could ever be free of him again.

He left then, angrily but silently, and she was alone, attacked by another fit of violent shivering.

The thing was, she thought feverishly as she secured the flat door, she had to stop loving him, she had to find a way, so that she didn't have to go through the horror of four years ago again. She couldn't face it, the waiting and wondering and worrying as bad as or worse than the knowing.

Never again!

Trying to be rational, and calm, she forced herself to remember that she had eaten nothing since breakfast that morning. She got herself a bowl of yoghurt from the fridge, but swallowing it made her feel even colder, so she ran a bath and lay in it for a long time, letting the warm water soothe the unaccustomed soreness of her body.

But her thoughts, her emotions, couldn't be soothed, remaining as chaotic as before. She had lied when she had told Grant she hated him. She loved him, but somehow she had to stop.

It was as simple as that, and yet infinitely complex. Her mind was still a whirling kaleidoscope of conflict when she went to bed later, and it was then that she realised just how difficult a task she had set herself. She had been Grant's from the beginning, and his possession of her tonight had sealed her fate.

Now her body was refreshed, even if her bruised mind and aching heart were not, and she wanted him again, wanted his hands and mouth on her, and the powerful movement of his body in hers. Her flesh was warm and receptive, her body yielding with its own remembrance, but now there was no man to fulfil its renewed hungering, no Grant.

She moaned aloud, in a mad moment of wishing she had not sent him away—but he would have gone anyway after tomorrow, to the mountain which took away all the men she loved.

She dragged herself to the Embassy in the morning, her pallor and fatigue hidden beneath a thicker layer of make-up than she usually applied, and somehow she got through the day without really knowing or later remembering how she had done so.

The farewell party for the British team was being held that night at the house of a married colleague, and Renata knew most of the junior staff were expected to attend, to swell the numbers and, presumably, show support for their compatriots.

She had intended simply not going and inventing some excuse tomorrow, but at the last minute, the perversity of her painful loving tempted her. She wanted to see Grant one last time, convinced as she was that he would never return to Kathmandu. She wouldn't speak to him, though, she thought; she would make it clear that she wanted nothing more to do with him.

She just wanted to look, for the last time.

Knowing that she was a fool, that she would only be torturing herself and prolonging the length of time it would take her to forget him, Renata was still unable to resist. They had been instructed to 'come casual', so she dressed in one of her less conservative outfits, loose midnight-blue silk pants in harem-style, worn beneath a big, baggy white silk shirt with a double belt and a loosely knotted blue tie.

She made up, noticing that last night had drawn shadows below her eyes, so she used a vivid lipstick and a liberal amount of blusher in the hope of distracting attention from them. Finally she brushed her freshly washed hair until it was a sheet of dark silk, drawing it up and back at one side with her mother-of-pearl clasp, the way she had worn it on the night when she and Grant had first spoken to each other.

She took a taxi, out of consideration for her high heels. The house was an attractive one with wood fences about a garden somewhat rank and lushly overgrown after the hot monsoon weather, so the party was being held in the large lounge although it was a warm evening with just a few billowy clouds scurrying across the dark night sky.

It had been a mistake to come, Renata realised the moment she set foot in the crowded room, her face growing closed, the habitual reserve in her eyes deepening to wariness.

There were too many memories here.

Bill Thurlow was looking at her in startled recognition after a few seconds of blankness, Leo Summers was staring as if he knew he should know her but couldn't place her, Harish Gupta and his petite, pretty wife Kumari were smiling in welcome . . .

And Grant. He stood not far away, looking a little surprised to see her, and Renata's heart and stomach went into lurching orbit as their eyes met, but her mask was in place and she managed to look at him blankly, refusing to give him the acknowledgement of a smile. She saw his face grow tight and hard with suppressed anger as she turned away, seeking the Embassy crowd.

'Ambassador'll be here later,' someone said.

'Drink, Renata,' someone else offered, their host's wife, and she accepted a gin and lime, flinching inwardly at the woman's look of sympathy, aware that many of the older members of staff knew who her father had been and would guess at the ordeal this was for her.

She stood lost, while groups formed about her and then broke up again, a series of constantly changing circles because everyone was being madly sociable.

She wanted to run away, but she shrank from the prospect of drawing attention to herself. She would have to finish her drink before she tried to slip discreetly away, only she supposed she ought to wait until after the Ambassador had looked in.

Oh God, why couldn't Grant move further away? She was so conscious of him standing there, just a couple of metres away, able to hear her stilted responses to whatever remarks various people addressed to her.

'Renata? Miss Renata?'

It was the Mingma she remembered, in his late thirties now, an unusually big man for a Sherpa, but graceful nevertheless, and he was regarding her with a watchful wariness that was blended with sympathy. Stiff-faced, she gazed back at him, and memory came flooding back. It was Mingma who had tried to comfort her at Thyangboche four years ago after the distressed leader of the expedition had broken the news to her; Mingma who had seen her frozen grief turn to hard-faced bitterness and from whom she had later fled hysterically when he had wanted to tell her about the accident in the belief that knowing the full facts would help her to bear her loss.

'Mingma . . .' she breathed.

'You are well?' he asked courteously.

Renata felt herself crumpling inwardly. He was one of Ang Tsering Lama's people, he had been a friend of his, and here he was cautiously treating her like a memsahib! She began to shake, her face suddenly as open and vulnerable as a child's, and seeing it, Mingma opened his arms to her.

Depositing her glass hastily on a convenient table, she fell into them, with a brief glimpse of Grant, on the periphery of her vision, looking shocked and startled.

'Oh, Mingma . . . Mingma!' She wasn't sure if she was laughing or crying, but there was a comfort she had long been missing in the hand that patted her shoulder.

She was vaguely conscious of a stir about them and

above the murmur of voices she heard one clearly, Bill
Thurlow's, she thought, explaining, 'Stephen Armstrong's daughter.'

Renata drew back and stood looking at Mingma,
holding his hands in hers.

'I wondered if it would be you when I saw the name,'
she told him. 'You're a Sirdar now, aren't you?'

He grinned. 'Yes.'

'Going high?' she asked, releasing his hands.

'No more summits for me,' he laughed. 'See, here is
one of our high-altitude Sherpas. Remember?'

Ang Phurba had joined them, greeting Renata with a
grave smile. He had been Ang Tsering Lama's best
friend, about the same age, his remote quietness
complementing the other's happy outgoing nature.

'Who are the other Sherpas?' she asked. 'Do I know
them?'

'Narbu, cook, and Ang Tharke, mail runner, I think
not,' Ang Phurba said thoughtfully. 'They join us in Sola
Khumbu. Also our other high-altitude Sherpa, Pemba
Norbu.'

'The girls like that one,' Mingma elaborated. 'Young,
enthusiastic. He wants to go high.'

The way Ang Tsering Lama had been. Darryl too.
Renata's face grew shuttered again as her mind drifted
back to the cruelty of it. They had both been such young
men, so confident, so ambitious.

Mingma touched her shoulder, knowing her thoughts.

'You should let them go, Renata.'

She drew a deep breath. 'I thought I had,' she told him
sadly. 'It's time, isn't it? Four years. Perhaps I have, but
forgetting is another matter. It's memory that makes the
future so frightening.'

'For all,' Ang Phurba agreed in his quiet way, his English not quite as fluent as Mingma's. 'But you came here tonight. Is a good thing, maybe. When they told us you were at the Embassy we wanted to visit you, but we thought maybe better not, maybe you would be unhappy to remember.'

Renata looked at them both with affection. 'When I first arrived tonight, I thought I'd made a terrible mistake,' she confessed candidly. 'But I'm glad now that I came, even if my reason for doing so was stupid and . . . and self-destructive.'

She stole another glance towards where she had last glimpsed Grant Fowler. He hadn't moved far, and he was standing watching her. He looked slightly pale, she thought, and his eyes were dark with a shocked questioning.

She was sorry then. She had tried to begin to tell him a couple of times last night, but he hadn't given her the chance, and later, after they had made love, when he might have listened, she had been in no state to tell him.

She turned back to the two Sherpas. 'How is the expedition getting to Sola Khumbu? It's too late to do the whole journey on foot and still get to Everest before the starting date.'

'Fly to Lukla, then hire porters and march,' Mingma enlightened her.

Renata knew the march, having gone as far as Thyangboche four years ago: Lukla to Namche Bazar in the heart of Sola Khumbu, the Everest region of the Himalaya, to Thyangboche, to Lobuje which, at fourteen thousand feet, was the last inhabited place on the way up to Everest and which, apart from mountaineers and

Sherpas, only the fittest of trekkers could reach and endure.

Renata and the two men fell into the sort of discussion she had once actually enjoyed before anything to do with mountaineering became anathema, swopping their theories about altitude sickness from which even Sherpas, accustomed to living at great heights, suffered; reminiscing about the stunning achievements of the brilliant Messner on the world's highest mountain, that first entirely oxygenless ascent with Habeler and two years later his solo dash from the Tibetan north; remembering other climbers including the Sherpas and sharing their admiration for Pertemba, one of the best of them all.

Occasionally, they dropped into Sherpa and Renata was pleased to discover how much she remembered after so long, as only her Nepali had had much practice in the last year.

Then, as Mingma paused in the middle of a sentence, Renata turned with a sense of foreboding, to find that Grant Fowler had joined them.

'Mingma, sorry to interrupt.' The smile he gave the Sherpa was strained, a mere courtesy. Then he looked at Renata. 'Renata, do you mind? I must talk to you, please.'

As she stood speechless and hesitant, Mingma looked from her to Grant with sudden understanding, and the smile he gave them was sympathetic.

'We'll see you again later, Renata,' he said, Ang Phurba supporting him with his silent, contained smile, and then the two were drifting away and she was left alone with Grant.

'Let's find ourselves some privacy,' he said curtly. 'I

think there's a side veranda through that door over there.'

'Grant . . .' For long seconds, Renata lacked the power of movement, lost in the cauldron of emotions his nearness awoke, a boiling, swirling conflict; wanting him, loving him, hating him . . .

'Please,' Grant said urgently, and she stirred herself, looking into the darkness of his eyes, seeing the disturbance in their depths and guessing how he must be feeling.

'All right,' she agreed faintly, and allowed him to lead her across the room and out through the door to the wooden-railed side veranda.

# CHAPTER SIX

RENATA stood at the wooden railing, acutely conscious of Grant just behind her. The warm yellow glow from the lantern-type light at the end of the veranda enveloped them, but in front of her the lush, jungly garden was in darkness, black against black.

'Why didn't you tell me?' Grant asked tautly after a few moments.

Searching for words, she turned to look at him. The yellow light made him look even darker, and she experienced a sharp, sensual tug of desire, seeing him in her mind as he had been in her bedroom last night, stripped of his casual clothes, shuddering with the force of passion.

'Why didn't you tell me who you were?' he demanded again.

'I'm sorry.' Her voice was just above a whisper. 'I don't know what to say. I . . . You see, before, when I didn't know who you were, there didn't seem any need to rush to tell you. It was just . . . part of my past, with no connection with the present or the future, and I wasn't ready to talk about it yet. Then, last night . . .'

'Last night I wouldn't listen and you were too distressed and incoherent to insist on my hearing you,' he supplied grimly. 'And now the silence rebounds on me, my silence about what I do and yours about your family . . . God, it's all so bloody bitterly ironical! You never talked about your father, so I guessed whatever memory you had of him was painful, but I restrained myself from probing since you so obviously felt it as over-possessiveness and an invasion of your privacy whenever I wanted to know your thoughts. I decided to wait for you to tell me of your own accord . . . I wish to hell now that I had asked you.'

'It . . . it has all rebounded on me too,' Renata offered in a tight, stifled voice, oppressed by the tragedy of it. She felt as sorry for him as she did for herself, knowing his anger stemmed from regret.

'Yes,' Grant agreed savagely. 'It's like a bad joke, isn't it? One of those cruel tricks of fate that occur so regularly in the old tragedies, but which you just don't anticipate in real, modern life. I never even connected the name, damn it. Armstrong isn't exactly uncommon, and it just never occurred to me that one of Stephen Armstrong's daughters would be working in Nepal. I suppose I just didn't think about it . . . Renata, you've mentioned your sister. Janine? Which of you was it who was here when your brother Darryl died?'

'Me,' she told him in a tiny voice.

'Then it was you who . . .' He paused, his mouth twisting. 'You were on the point of becoming engaged to Ang Tsering, weren't you?'

'Ang Tsering Lama,' she pronounced, suddenly resenting the European habit of not knowing the full names of Sherpas. 'I was waiting for them at Thyangboche and . . . they never came.'

She saw him wince and knew he was remembering his suggestion that she wait for him at Thyangboche.

He said heavily, 'I suppose I might have made the connection if I'd been made aware of the accident at the time it happened, but . . . I'd been avalanched on K2 and

I was unconscious in an Islamabad hospital, so I didn't learn of it until weeks later, and by then people had stopped talking about it. I just heard the bare outlines, that the pair had died and that Armstrong's sister had been in love with Ang Tsering and was . . . embittered by her double loss. I never heard anything more. It was too long afterwards.'

'Of course,' Renata agreed tartly, the old bitterness rising acridly.

'Don't!' Grant said sharply. 'I've enough imagination to understand how you feel, and knowing my fellow-climbers, they'd have been concerned for you, but there wouldn't have been much any of us could do if you'd deliberately cut yourself off from them, and that's what you did, isn't it?'

'And do you understand that, Grant?' she challenged resentfully. 'Do you understand why we did it, my mother and I, why I swore I'd never wait for another man to come down from a mountain?'

'Oh yes, I understand,' he assured her expressionlessly.

'And I suppose you think I'm a coward?' she retaliated, hurt by something, she wasn't sure what.

'God, do you really believe I'm so insensitive?' Grant exploded furiously, but when he went on it was in a tone flat with resignation: 'Yes, well, perhaps you do after the way I refused to listen or understand last night. But knowing the facts, I understand now, Renata. You lost people you loved——'

'Three men in three years,' she supplied dully. 'I never want to feel that fear again, or . . . or what came afterwards when I knew they were dead. Never again.'

'I know. Your loss was too great, wasn't it? More than anyone can be expected to bear,' Grant said quite gently,

but he sounded weary as well, as if drained of emotion.
'I'd met your father and brother. We all mourned their
deaths; they were among the best. Your father actually
had a lot to do with my starting to climb. I heard him
lecture when I was a kid and he was at the height of his
fame, in his prime . . . His words, his descriptions, made
me want to go out and try it.'

'Oh, God,' Renata said hollowly.

'I'm sorry, I shouldn't have told you that,' Grant
realised flatly. 'As for Ang Tsering, you must know how
highly he was regarded. He was with me on Cho Oyu the
spring before his death; he got to the top . . . He was a
brilliant climber.

'He was a brilliant human being,' Renata said
savagely.

'Yes, I know,' Grant affirmed quietly. 'To the
mountaineering world, his death was a tragedy; but your
personal tragedy was even greater—I realise that. You
must have loved him very much.'

Grant had mentioned tragedies earlier, but Renata
suddenly found herself wondering hysterically if that was
wrong. There was an aspect of comedy here after all—
black comedy. The realisation hit her anew. These men,
these climbers, were a different breed. Nothing and no
one could mean more than the game. Almost in horror
she stared at Grant, and yet at the same time she was
absorbing the savage humour of the truth, and wanting
to laugh, but any laughter would have had an hysterical
ring. This was the man who had been so possessive,
darkly jealous of Wes Davies and even the toilet seat
salesman she had told him about; yet now she could
detect no trace of jealousy with regard to Ang Tsering
Lama, and she knew why. He had been part of the game,

a fellow climber and, as such, held in higher regard than any woman could be.

'Renata——' Grant was continuing urgently, but at that moment they were joined on the veranda by the Guptas.

'My apologies for intruding,' the aristocratic-looking Harish offered. 'But I told Ben I'd see if I could find you. The Ambassador has just arrived, Grant, and he would like a few words before he has to go to an affair at the palace. Miss Armstrong, my apologies to you too. It's good to see you again.'

Grant touched Renata's shoulder, his face darkening as she flinched from the contact.

'I still have things to say to you, so don't go away,' he instructed, adding urgently, 'Please!'

But there was nothing left to say, she reflected desolately, watching him re-enter the house before turning and greeting the Guptas.

'It has been too long,' Harish reproached her gently. 'But . . . You're back now? You and Grant Fowler . . .?'

'No. It was a mistake, I'm afraid,' Renata said sadly, and thought—what a mistake!

'I'm sorry. Come, shall we follow him in?' Harish was too polite to probe.

Renata looked at his wife Kumari enviously. She was lucky. Harish would go to Everest, but he wasn't a climber. As liaison officer he would remain at base camp, in relative safety.

Inside, Renata found herself trapped. Bill Thurlow came over to renew his acquaintance, followed by Leo Summers, the bearded expedition doctor who specialised in researching such high altitude ailments as pulmonary and cerebral oedema. Before she had a chance to escape,

Mingma and Ang Phurba had joined their group and shortly afterwards she found herself being introduced to the other team members.

Pirie Jones, a dreamy-eyed Cornishman, was the only one she hadn't seen before, she realised. Ben Anderson, a university lecturer from Scotland, she recognised as the man who had been with Grant at the Annapurna on the night they had met, and Pat Fiore had been his companion at the monkey temple the first time she had seen him. Pat was younger than the others; like so many great mountaineers, he came from Manchester, and Renata's long experience of the breed recognised a climber in the tradition of Whillans and Brown, the first of the brilliant post-war 'hard men' of climbing.

It was his first time in Nepal, and Renata used the fact to initiate a conversation which she hoped would exclude the subject of climbing. Soon, to her relief, they were discussing the rights and wrongs of the apprenticing of very young children to such local crafts as carpet-making, but part of her remained conscious of Grant, first talking to the Ambassador and now, released, moving purposefully towards them.

She could feel herself stiffening with wary resentment, and it became difficult to concentrate on what was being asked of her.

'I think you have to judge Nepal by its own standards, or at least by Asian standards,' she managed, apt to be defensive because she still loved this country. It's a poor country.'

She was aware of Grant, right beside her now, but he made no attempt to interrupt as Pat Fiore laughed.

'Determined to get richer! Can you guess the massive

fee the Nepalese government is charging us for Everest?
It's unbelievable!'

'I can imagine, but it's obvious, isn't it? Here they
have a natural resource for which there's a worldwide
demand, the Himalaya; they'd be fools not to put a high
price on them. Believe me, the poverty is real. Haven't
you heard the joke about Nepal's biggest export to India
being the soil that's washed away by the rivers? That sort
of thing makes the situation serious. So tourism is the
biggest industry, though still developing, and if people
like you are prepared to pay fortunes to try to climb their
mountains and——'

Her resentment of the thing that drove them all had
been rising, her voice growing hard and tight as she went
on, but the steely fingers closing round her arm brought
her to an abrupt halt before she could do the unforgivable
and spill her anguish and bitterness all over them in an
outburst of angry despair.

'Excuse us, will you?' Grant addressed the others
pleasantly. 'Renata and I were interrupted earlier and
we've got a conversation to finish ... A personal
conversation.'

'Finish is the word,' she muttered furiously when they
were out on the veranda again. 'Grant, there's nothing
more to say.'

'I suppose you're right,' he said, releasing her, but her
arm continued to burn beneath the silk sleeve. 'But I
didn't want you saying what you were about to say and
having Pat and the others go to Everest with the memory
of it in their minds.'

'Why not?' Renata flared angrily. 'Why shouldn't they
be made aware of what it does to women when men are
stupid enough to go to mountains and push themselves

beyond all reasonable limits and suffer incredible
hardships and at best come back with frostbite but more
probably remain there as frozen corpses? Why
shouldn't——'

'I understand that you're apt to be emotional about it,'
Grant cut in. 'But you're also the daughter and sister of
two great mountaineers, Renata. Underneath all that
hurt, you understand as well as anyone.'

The rage went out of her and she stood looking at him
helplessly.

'Yes, it's just something,' she confirmed bleakly.
'Something there inside you. That's why there's nothing
to say, Grant.'

His eyes flashed. 'You may have nothing to say, but
I've changed my mind. I have plenty.' He paused. 'Your
faith in the consistency of fate or whatever is amazing;
we all know how unpredictable it can be, and how
ironical too. Is it likely you'll lose anyone else in the same
way again? There's an equal chance of my losing you.
You could step under a bus one day, or the Embassy
could become caught up in some terrorist activity as even
Nepal hasn't escaped the violent solution syndrome. It's
a chance I'll take.'

Suddenly Renata was laughing weakly because again
it was so typical of the breed. 'Oh, fate and chance! Yes.
But Grant, you're forgetting. I know the odds.'

He didn't share her laughter. 'It's a bloody mess, isn't
it? By our reticence about the facts of our lives, we've
created this . . . this! Renata, I do know what I've done to
you, and it can't be undone. I wish to God I'd known who
you were, how you felt. I'd have left you alone then. But I
didn't, and you fell in love with me, and now it's too late.'

'Not necessarily,' she disagreed promptly. 'The answer

is obvious. I'll just have to fall out of love with you.'

'Can you?' he countered sardonically. 'Last night, you said you hated me, but somehow I don't think it's true.'

'Yes,' she conceded smartly. 'But I want to stop loving you—I've got to! I want to be indifferent to you . . .'

'Can you?' he asked again.

'I have to,' Renata asserted emphatically.

'And last night?'

'Was . . . an experience,' she allowed, before abandoning the act. 'Oh, Grant, I didn't know . . . I didn't know it . . . could be like that.'

'Nor did I,' he responded ironically. 'I've never felt so close to a woman before, so much part of her. It was as if you took my soul into you along with my body . . . Oh, believe me, Renata, if I've caused you suffering, I've wounded myself as severely. I want you so badly, I'll always want you, and to know you still feel similarly . . . God! What do you want of me?'

Renata's face became hard and closed as she regarded him silently, but her eyes glinted. It wouldn't even occur to him that he was giving her the opening to ask him not to climb. She could imagine how shocked he would be were she to do so . . . Only she couldn't. She was an Armstrong, the daughter and sister of mountain men, and she knew the rules, as she knew the men. Grant was the same.

It was the same old story. He could no more stop climbing than he could voluntarily cease breathing; it was easier, more natural, to give up a woman. He wanted her, he might even love her in a second-best way, but he could never give her the total commitment with which other unflawed men, the ones who didn't need to climb mountains, loved their women.

What she had intended as a sardonic laugh emerged as a gasp of pain.

'Oh, Grant, you just don't know, do you? The worst of it, the very worst . . . Will there ever be a man to whom a woman means even more than the compulsion to go high? We can't compete, can we? The mountains win every time.'

To her surprise, Grant seemed to hesitate, and the look he gave her was oddly resentful, almost hostile. She supposed he didn't like hearing the truth. He could even feel a little guilty, or inadequate, because he was not able to love as other men did, wholly and exclusively.

Then he said sharply, 'If that's your view, there doesn't seem much left to say. We've been through this, we've agreed that it can't be properly or fully explained——'

'What obsession can?' Renata retorted. 'You see, you see why it's no use! I can't have one of you in my life again, I can't face it.'

'I know, I know.' Grant was suddenly impatient and she knew that now he was anxious to escape before she started making the demands to which he could never accede. But he forced himself to continue, reluctantly, 'Renata, if you're pregnant . . .?'

'Oh, God!' The possibility hadn't occurred to her before, but now she beheld it as the worst fate imaginable. 'Oh, God, no! I couldn't bear it, I just couldn't. I saw how my mother looked when Darryl died and . . . a child of yours would want to climb too.'

'The wish to do so might conceivably come from your side,' snapped Grant. 'Your genes can't be entirely innocent of whatever it is, considering who your father and brother were. Renata, if you are pregnant——'

'I can't be! I mustn't be!' She was almost hysterical at the prospect.

'Are you saying you'd contemplate abortion?' A steely note had entered his voice. 'Termination of pregnancy is the delicate expression, I believe.'

The idea hadn't crossed her mind, but panic made her lash out, 'It would be my right.'

'It would be my child.'

'The choice is mine.'

'No!' Grant's protest was like the crack of a rifle and he had grasped by her shoulders, his fingers biting mercilessly into her flesh. 'For God's sake, Renata, spare me that. All right, I'll accept that I've got to get out of your life, but if there's a child, someone I've helped you create, I can't let it be destroyed. Promise me! Promise me that if you're pregnant you'll contact me when I get back to Kathmandu.'

'If you get back,' she inserted acidly, but she could feel tears smarting at the back of her eyes as she looked up into his face, dark, angry and unhappy. She still loved him, and however much she was suffering now, he couldn't be feeling much happier.

'Renata——'

'All right,' she assured him on a sigh. 'If I do turn out to be pregnant and if you do come back, we can discuss it together. But please God I won't be. If I don't contact you, you'll know it's all right.'

'It will never be all right!' Suddenly there was a change in his mood; his voice had harshened and he was drawing her close against him with fierce, bruising strength. 'There's so much here between us, such strength of feeling, it can't just end like this. I won't let it!'

He was shaking against her and Renata felt the warm weakness of response invading her loins.

'It must,' she choked as a tear spilled down her cheek. 'You know that—you've said you understand.'

'No!' Grant protested violently. 'I can't accept it. You belong to me. How can you deny it?'

'Grant——' She tried to free herself, but he held her with an easy, ruthless strength and her body, held fast against his, was remembering the way it had been last night, the power of his possession, and the rapture it had created.

'You said you loved me, but if you can walk away from what we've got, then you don't love me enough,' he accused angrily, resentment twisting his mouth.

He was so wrong, she thought despairingly. She loved him too much, even more than she had loved Ang Tsering Lama, she admitted. She loved him too much to be able to endure his being part of her life, because the terror for him would be greater than before, a burden too intolerably heavy for her strength.

'I want to love you less,' she reminded him brokenly, and saw his anger recede.

'Yes, of course,' he remembered reluctantly. 'I suppose I'm . . . being selfish. No reasonable person could expect you to commit yourself to a mountaineer when you've lost so much already, and I hate myself for what I've done to you . . . For your sake, I suppose I have to hope you get over it quickly, forget me . . . But God, it's hard, Renata, to have to accept that this is the end, when we could have had so much.'

'I know. I'm sorry.' She wasn't sure what she was apologising for; for having old wounds, or was it for being a coward? 'Let me go now, Grant, let me start the forgetting.'

'I can't,' he groaned. 'I must at least kiss you one last time. Oh God, Renata!'

His mouth was on hers, covering it, and Renata had neither strength nor will to resist the impelling possessiveness of his kiss, trembling against his hardness, held tightly to him by the iron strength of the arms about her.

It was a kiss of despair, of almost frenzied desperation, mouths locked, grinding together, as if they both sought to deny the inevitable, to stave off the moment of parting.

Grant's hands moved on her back, his rough caresses running the length of her body, from shoulder to thigh, and Renata clung to him in an agony of love and need. Her breasts were swollen, her hips jerked uncontrollably against him as the secret flesh at the centre of her femininity which had known the fierce caress of his manhood last night responded urgently and tender sensation swiftly became the throbbing ache of hunger.

She was moaning softly when he freed her mouth. Somehow she forced her body to cease its erotic writhing against the hardness of his, but her senses were still clamant with desire for him, her flesh hotly sensitive. Grant was murmuring inarticulately against the satin smoothness of her slenderly fragile neck, drawing back a little to lay one slightly trembling hand over her breast. His touch scorched her through the silk of her shirt and she gave a low cry of mingled frustration and pleasure as he touched the tautly thrusting nipple.

'Renata, is there no way?' he demanded urgently, but in the next instant his face grew shuttered, and she wondered why.

'I can't,' she answered him achingly.

'I wish there was some way I could overcome this fear of yours.'

'I know too much, I've lost too much,' Renata responded sadly.

'And you can't even give me tonight, this one last night, can you?' he challenged.

'It would only make it even more difficult to let go afterwards.' Her swollen lips trembled and tears were threatening again.

'For both of us, I think,' Grant agreed slowly, releasing her. 'God, I almost hope you are pregnant; then you'll have to see me again . . . have me in your life.'

'No.'

'This is all, then? Are you coming inside?'

'I'll stay out here a while, I think.'

He stood looking at her in the soft yellow light for a time. He said, 'How do I say goodbye?'

There was a constriction in Renata's throat and she swallowed painfully.

'I don't know what to say either,' she told him unevenly. 'I used to say all the right things to the others, all the little formulae for good luck and safety and success, but they didn't work. But by the time your expedition is over, safely or otherwise, I hope I'll have stopped caring.'

'Renata.' He lifted a hand to touch her face, the lightest of caresses, only his fingertips brushing her cheek.

'Let's not say anything,' she pleaded in a jerky whisper. 'Just go, Grant. Walk away from me.'

'Yes.'

He was curt, inclining his head, once, before turning

and leaving her, and the last glimpse she had of his face revealed a taut, dark mask, resolutely schooled, though the eyes remained stormy.

Renata watched him go, convinced that she would never see him again. How could she, when Everest took all those she loved?

Renata remained on the veranda for a time, wanting to be sure she had herself well under control before re-entering the house. She leaned against the wooden railing, allowing her mind to drift over all that had passed between Grant and herself this evening, knowing that such an indulgence would contribute nothing to the restoration of her composure but too weak-willed to help herself.

In a moment of anger, he had accused her of not loving him enough, but it was his love that was insufficient, she reflected. If he loved her at all, and she couldn't be sure that he did, because he had never said so, then he certainly didn't love her enough. He would make no sacrifices for her. Instead, he would sacrifice her.

Once again, the mountains had defeated her, and without even taking a life yet, this time; once again, she had lost.

It wasn't really the mountains, though, she acknowledged bleakly. Mountains were beautiful, the Himalaya still the most breathtaking sight she had ever seen in her life. They were lovely to look at, and she had once taken an academic interest in the problems they presented to those who climbed them and the various methods of overcoming those difficulties, although she had never felt a personal need to go high, being content merely to look.

But it was simpler to hate something as solid and

substantial as a mountain range than to blame that mysterious, inexplicable spirit which drove some men to climb.

Renata grew impatient with her thoughts. Analysis, dissection; they couldn't alter the facts. She understood the situation and knew that it was unchangeable. She had to face it, accept it, and start training herself not to think about Grant. She had to forget the man, to teach her body to forget him and harden her heart. From now on, the only way life was going to be endurable was if she could stop loving and needing him; to go on and on, haunted by him through the years, whether he was living or dead would be intolerable. She had to gain some measure of freedom from him simply to be able to go on living.

She was under no illusions about the difficulty of her task. She loved in a way she had not loved before, and she had no memory of another man's possession to obliterate or substitute for the memory of his. To begin with, she knew it was going to be a slow and agonisingly painful process, a gradual schooling of herself during which both heart and body would often betray her.

As she re-entered the house, a quick glance told her that both the Ambassador and his wife, plus all the expedition members, had departed. Renata kept her face averted as she crossed the room, sensing curious glances and suspecting that her face must betray her, her lips still swollen from Grant's kiss and denuded of the bright lipstick she had worn earlier.

She murmured what she suspected was an unintelligible farewell to her host and hostess and slipped away, walking a couple of blocks until a taxi cruised past and she stopped it.

At her flat, she faced another sleepless night. She had intended to start her cure tonight and practise not thinking about Grant, but it was hopeless. He kept intruding and eventually she gave up trying, despising herself for being weak-willed but devoid of the energy necessary for the effort.

She would begin tomorrow, she promised herself, feeling some shame but more relief as she gave up the fight. Just for tonight she would indulge herself and let thoughts of Grant fill her mind.

They could not be happy thoughts, though, when already she had lost him to the mountains. Consequently, she was mourning him, she realised.

She had gone to bed, and as she lay in the darkness she discovered that there were tears on her face, which shocked her because she hadn't noticed she was crying.

She found herself contemplating what her life would be from now on. Empty was the description which occurred most readily. Her existence would be just that, a meaningless and lonely process of existing because she lacked the courage to face again the strain and terror of sharing her life with a man who spent much of his time on mountains.

But, if only she could stop loving him, the emptiness would be preferable to the fear on which she had turned her back. Anything would be. That was why she had made that vow—never again.

She didn't think it possible that there might be a third man in her life. She had had two chances of happiness with two different men, so very different and yet both flawed by the fatal urge which destroyed the happiness. She would not be given another chance, and if she was ... A gasp of tearful laughter choked Renata. She was flawed too. Either that, or she was simply fated to love climbers. How could Grant have said fate was unpredictable? It, or her heart's choices, had proved one hundred per cent consistent, regarding the men she loved.

But she knew she wouldn't love again, her reasoning given ballast by a deeper conviction which she shrank from admitting for fear of despairing utterly if she did so.

Grant Fowler was not going to be exorcised. Her love for him could not be uprooted or destroyed; nor would time and distance cause it to evaporate. It was with her for all time, undying, and she would never be free of it. She could only bury it and know that it would always be there to betray her.

# CHAPTER SEVEN

BACK-PACKS were a familiar sight in Kathmandu, starting point for so many trekkers, but the partially obscured figure was familiar, and Renata quickened her pace and overtook her.

'Karen? Have you just got back?'

'Ren!' Karen Richards stopped and heaved a sigh. 'A day later than I promised, so I'm probably in a heap of trouble. Can you believe, I missed two flights from Lukla and then at this end I missed the bus from the airport and had to walk.'

'Let me help you,' Renata offered, but Karen laughed.

'There's only the H-frame, and you're looking too elegant for that. I can make it. Are you on your way home? Why not come to my place for a while and tell me what's new in Kathmandu?'

'All right,' Renata agreed, grateful for the prospect of company. The evenings had stretched long and lonely just recently. 'How was it?'

'Great,' Karen assured her as they fell into step. 'Though I will say I've had a surfeit of hiking. It will last me a while, I think, so if we decide to do anything this weekend, let's make it cycling and to hell with the expense. Sola Khumbu is gorgeous at this time of year, though I had a few wet days with no visibility, the tail end of the monsoon. Alec and Wes sent their love, by the way. I spent a couple of nights with Alec before leaving.'

'You're looking well on it,' Renata commented,

admiring her friend's deep tan and the way the sun had streaked her golden-brown hair.

'What, the hiking or Alec?' laughed Karen.

'Well, I don't suppose Alec gave you that suntan!'

'Right! I was wondering, by the way—is it just in contrast to me that you look paler than I recall!'

'Oh . . . I don't know,' Renata offered feebly. She knew she looked terrible these days with dark circles beneath her eyes and a lack of colour in her cheeks, and there were days when she felt too listless to make more than a minimum effort with her make-up.

'What's wrong?' Karen demanded. 'Have you been sick? You're too experienced to let yourself in for Kathmandu tummy, surely?'

'No, I'm fine, really.' Renata forced a smile, still undecided about whether to confide in her or not, and if it would serve any purpose if she did so. She was supposed to be forgetting, not remembering.

'If you say so,' Karen returned sceptically.

'Tell me about Sola Khumbu,' Renata requested to distract her.

'I thought you hated all mention of that region? Hey, that reminds me! Too bad about the hunk.'

'The hunk?'

'The one you were aiming to pull in the Annapurna after the men and I left that last night we ate together,' Karen reminded her. 'I bet you got out fast when you discovered who he was.'

Renata's step faltered and a spasm of pain crossed her face.

'I didn't discover who he was until . . . it was too late,' she confessed dully.

Karen stopped walking and stared at her. 'Now, that's

a very interesting statement, Renata. What happened? Do you mean you had an affair? Fell in love?'

Renata closed her eyes momentarily as if to shut out a memory.

'He didn't tell me who he was and I didn't know,' she repeated in the same lifeless voice.

'He's really hurt you, hasn't he?' Karen realised, seeing the bruised look in her eyes and the way her vulnerable mouth shook. 'The bastard! Why didn't he tell you, d'you know? Did he know who you were? Is that why he kept silent?'

'No. We both . . . There were things we didn't tell each other, that . . . that rebounded on us both.'

'Come on, let's get to my apartment and you can tell me about it, if you feel like talking. Discussing it might make you feel better and anyway, I'm curious,' Karen concluded candidly.

'How . . . how did you find out?' Renata questioned her as they resumed walking.

'That he's the leader of the post-monsoon British expedition to Everest? I came across them in Sola Khumbu. We were going in opposite directions, but there was a heavy session of *chang*-drinking going on in the village where we were all spending the night and I was invited to join them.'

'How . . . was he? Did he look——' Renata forced herself to stop. She wasn't helping herself this way, but dear God, she was so hungry for news of him.

Karen looked at her sympathetically. 'It's really bad, isn't it? Sorry, hon, but I didn't exchange a word with him. The invitation came from a younger hunk called Pat Fiore and an even younger and very handsome Sherpa called Pemba Norbu. Mr Grant Fowler barely noticed me, and not for want of trying on my part. I figured you'd have lost interest when you found out who he was and that all was fair, as they say. But nothing doing! I can tell you, I felt pretty chagrined. He just looked right through me and didn't even crack a smile, not once! We were in this house . . . You know what the village houses are like there? He sat there, and it's my belief that he was trying, in a calculated, systematic way, to get dead drunk. But it didn't work. By the time the party broke up, he was as sober as when he started drinking. I know, because I was waiting to see him fall flat on his face, but he just walked out of there stone cold sober. It was amazing, because that *chang* is pretty potent stuff. But I ask you, is that an appropriate frame of mind in which to be going to Everest?'

'Oh, it won't matter once they're there, on the mountain,' Renata told her with a faint, bitter laugh. 'Then, everything extraneous is forgotten, personal problems, families, the lot. Nothing matters then.'

'And you hate it, don't you?' Karen looked at her curiously. 'You seem to think or to know that he had a reason for wanting to get plastered. Was he in love with you?'

'He wanted me,' Renata said curtly.

'Oh. And did——'

'Yes,' Renata cut in sharply.

Karen asked no further questions for a while after that, sensing her reluctance to elaborate, but later when they had reached their destination and were seated in Karen's kitchen with mugs of soup Renata told her most of the story.

She spoke in that quiet, dead tone that betrayed her utter despair, the lack of all hope that had taken all the sparkle from her eyes, leaving them like dark empty wells. Renata didn't cry any more. She had done all her crying during that first tormented night after her final parting with Grant, and she had no more tears left to shed.

'And that's it?' said Karen when she came to a halt.

'Most of it.' There were some things that couldn't be shared.

Karen was silent, reviewing the sad little tale. Then she asked, 'Well, why didn't you just ask him to quit climbing?'

Renata stared at her, startled, until she recalled that Karen must have had little contact with mountaineering people until coming to Nepal.

She shrugged and explained, 'I couldn't. It's just not something anyone does. It would make no difference, anyway . . . Climbing is a compulsion. Oh, I can't explain it, and neither can the ones who climb, though they try on occasion.'

'It's not simply a case of—because it's there?'

Renata smiled. 'No. It's more than that. It's not simply anything. It's very complex and totally mysterious.'

'Like something that comes from the soul? I have to admit, those climbers I've met have convinced me that they're a breed apart,' Karen confided. 'They all seem to have this restless vitality. Dynamic, sort of. They're all pretty charismatic, even when they're sitting trying to get drunk. But look, you say it's not done, to ask a man to quit, but rules are for breaking.'

'It's more than a rule, it's a taboo. My mother never asked my father,' Renata remembered. 'But don't you see, Karen? I can't take it again, I can't commit myself to Grant, and the obvious solution, if we want to be

together, is for him to stop climbing. But that simply
didn't occur to him. That's how I know he doesn't care
enough, that he probably doesn't really love me. He just
wants me.'

'He looks intelligent enough, so you'd think it would
occur to him. It's a mess, isn't it?'

'He said once that I didn't love him enough,' Renata
recalled. 'I suppose it could look that way, but it's not
that. Perhaps I'm crazy or a coward, but I love him too
much to be able to take losing him that way, on a
mountain.'

'It's not crazy or cowardly when your past is taken into
consideration,' Karen assured her warmly. 'You've lost
too much already. It's only natural that you should have a
sort of phobia.'

'I'd rather lose him this way that I've chosen,' Renata
went on. 'By trying to forget him, stop loving him.'

'But can you do that? You don't look as if you've been
having much success so far.' Karen inspected her
thoughtfully. 'I don't know what to suggest. Another
man wouldn't help yet, I guess. Incidentally, it's
beginning to look as if Wes is serious about his Sherpani.'

Sensitively, Renata felt she had imposed enough on
Karen with her personal problems, so she responded to
the introduction of a new topic, and Grant Fowler wasn't
mentioned again until she left to return to her own flat a
bit later.

Then Karen said, 'I wish I could help, Renata, but I've
never been much good at relationships myself. That's
why this thing I've got with Alec suits me, because it
can't really be called a relationship. But I've cried my
share, and I know the value of doing so . . . So any time

you need a shoulder, or just an ear, don't have any inhibitions. Okay?'

'Thanks, Karen.' This time Renata didn't have to force a smile. 'But let's hope it can only get better from now on.'

'From the look of you, it can't get much worse,' Karen retorted. 'That's not mascara under your eyes, is it? You're going to end up looking like a panda if you're not careful. Hell, Ren, I still think you should have asked him to quit for your sake.'

'How could I?' Renata returned helplessly. 'And anyway, he couldn't have pulled out of Everest.'

'Why the hell not?'

'Well, he was committed to it, obviously. People were relying on him——'

'So why shouldn't he switch his allegiance and commit himself to you?' Suddenly Karen began to laugh. 'You know. I was thinking you were soft, but it's not that after all. You're still one of them, you think like them. You may imagine you've cut yourself off from the world of climbing, but you still belong. Grant Fowler is committed to Everest, so you've got no claim on him. My God, I could never think like that in a million years, but then we don't produce too many mountaineers in Fort Lauderdale.'

Her comments gave Renata something to think about as she walked home. She supposed there were certain things she took for granted, aspects of climbing that seemed unalterable. It was inevitable, with her upbringing in a mountaineering family. Without ever having been verbally taught to her, a creed or a code had become ingrained, and her four years' isolation had done nothing to eradicate it.

Alone in her flat, however, her mind turned inexorably to Grant. It was like this every evening, missing him, wanting him, and it never got any better.

She had been a fool to think she could stop loving him, but now it was beginning to look as if she wasn't even capable of burying her love. It was with her constantly, hurting her. There was no forgetting, no easing of the pain; just endless unhappiness and a dark sense of futility.

Worst of all were the nights, when she lay in the bed where he had claimed her, making her his—as she so undeniably was. She would never be free of him, she suspected. Without the consent of her mind, her heart and her woman's body had made their commitment to one man, and only that one, for all time.

Her plan to train herself not to want him wasn't working. Unhappiness and physical frustration broke into her sleep, twin demons that were destroying her.

And through it all, fear ate at her, the fear she had hoped to avoid by the swift interment of her love for Grant and the reason for her inability to share her life with him.

She knew too much. At first there was little news, but she knew the route up to Everest—Lukla, Namche Bazar, Thyangboche of her worst memory, Lobuje, and then the base camp—and she could make guesses at their pace.

She had never been on Everest, of course, though she had been to it, and flown over it four years ago, but her knowledge of it came mostly from her father because his last climb had not been his first attempt nor even his first time on the summit. More than anyone she knew, Stephen Armstrong had been obsessed with that one

particular mountain, and he had passed his knowledge to
his children.

Renata could visualise it from all sides, but the aspect
she knew best was that leading to the original route and
to the South-West Face, which was the way Grant and
his team were attempting. They were constantly there in
her mind when the news came that the expedition had set
up base camp: the Ice Fall, one of the most dangerous
bits of work in climbing the mountain, the Western Cwm
between Everest and Nuptse, the stubbornly difficult
rock band . . .

She had hoped to have reached a stage where she could
ignore the drama that was taking place on Everest, as she
had ignored other mountaineering dramas in recent
years, but instead she found that she sought news, driven
even to ringing the Nepalese Ministry of Tourism
because all news, especially of a successful ascent, was
required to be sent first to that department, which then
announced it; also she never missed a weather report.

In the Himalaya, even a semi-Alpine-style ascent was
a long affair, and even longer for those not involved, with
nothing to do but wait for tidings. The days became
weeks and anxiety gnawed ceaselessly at Renata.
Brought up as she had been, she was aware of every
danger that threatened climbers, of those moments of
peril which could snuff out a life in seconds. A slip, a fall,
and a roped climber might take his companion with him
if the latter's reaction was a fraction of a second too slow;
the same went for avalanches. She knew well the danger
of passing by the huge seracs in the Ice Fall, of a lip that
might break off and pitch a man into a crevasse, of falling rock, of the extreme weather conditions, especially
the jet-stream winds at this time of year, of being

benighted . . . How many men had simply disappeared on Everest, men glimpsed heading for the summit and never seen again, beginning with those first two more than sixty years ago? And those who were left could only guess and speculate as to what had happened.

She could only wait, and it was destroying her. This was what she had known she could not endure and why she had wanted Grant out of her life, and yet, ironically, she was still having to endure it because she had been unable to stop loving Grant or even to sublimate her love.

She ought to hate Grant for forcing her to endure this, yet it was only because she loved him that she was having to do so; living perpetually in dread of his death and yet knowing she could never share his life.

The day came when she knew for certain that she was not pregnant. The knowledge should have brought relief, considering her earlier panic, but her reaction was strangely ambivalent. She didn't want a child, Grant's child, who would one day want to climb mountains, and yet if Grant were to die, a child would be a living part of him that was left behind, for her to cherish in his memory.

A spasm of self-disgust had gripped her as she realised what she was thinking. That was sick! A child was an individual human being, never a monument to a man. It was just as well that there was no child, if she had sunk this low.

News came more regularly now, but it was bad news to begin with. Pirie Jones had frostbite and had descended to advance base camp where Leo Summers was attending him. Fortunately, it seemed unlikely that he would need to lose anything. Then Pemba Norbu, the younger of the high-altitude Sherpas, descending for a while because of altitude sickness, was struck by a falling rock. Mercifully, he had remained conscious and been able to make his way down, but the expedition was over for him now.

'What bad luck for him,' Karen commented when Renata told her this. 'I liked him when I met him in Sola Khumbu, and he was so eager to make his mark.'

'It's good luck,' Renata retorted drily. 'He's unlikely to die this time.'

The team were being plagued by wind, it was learned next. As leader, Grant Fowler had attempted to put Ben Anderson and Pat Fiore on top, but the wind had forced them down, and they had now retreated to a lower camp for a rest.

Renata knew that a next attempt would probably involve Grant himself. She was sick that night, her stomach the first part of her to give in to the strain under which she was living.

Her mind would probably go next, she thought sardoncially, wondering if she could have developed an ulcer in just a few weeks or if she was simply turning into a hypochondriac. But they were endless weeks, seemingly, when they were filled with waiting and worrying. She couldn't bear much more.

Then, two days later, there was jubilation at the Embassy.

'They've made it!' one of the men was telling everyone he saw. 'Grant Fowler and Ang Phurba, on top!'

But it wasn't over yet, Renata thought, unsmiling. There was still the descent, and apparently there was to be another attempt at putting Anderson and Fiore on the summit so Grant might not come right down, through the Ice Fall, immediately.

There was no relief, then, and yet in the midst of the continuing coldness of her fear, she recognised a tiny area of warmth that was pride. It didn't surprise her. She might have cut herself off from mountaineering, she might have learnt to hate it, but she was still an Armstrong, capable of respecting great achievements; she was also a woman in love, and it was her man who was the achiever this time.

Ben Anderson and Pat Fiore succeeded in their second summit bid, and not long afterwards the news reached Kathmandu that the entire team had reached base camp in safety and were about to begin the trek down.

That evening, Karen Richards called at her flat and found Renata virtually cataleptic, hardly capable of moving or speaking.

'Hey, what's this zombie stuff?' she demanded as Renata sat down on the couch after admitting her. 'I've heard the news and it's all good! They've been up, they've got down and they're on their way back to Kathmandu. It's over, Ren.'

'Until the next time.' Renata's voice emerged as a thin thread of sound as she forced herself to respond. 'He once said something about a winter attempt on Lhotse, and after that there'll be other mountains, here, and in Pakistan, and a day will come when he'll turn to Everest again and want to try one of the routes from the other side, the north or the north-east. I feel worse now than I did before. I don't know, I suppose there was something inside me that was holding on until this was over . . . I probably fooled myself into thinking that would be the end of it, but it isn't. Why can't I stop loving him? I can't live with him, but it seems I can't live without him either. It's the original, classic situation, isn't it?'

Karen was regarding her with her head on one side. 'At a guess, I'd say you're heading for some kind of breakdown. You should hear yourself, that faraway voice, absolutely dead, and you should see yourself. Something has got to give! Oh, Ren, I feel so bad that there's nothing I can do to help, but you've made me realise it's a world I don't understand, your mountaineering. The rules are different, I guess. Well, I can't help or advise you, but I can do my best to cheer you up. I was thinking we could treat ourselves to a meal at the Yak and Yeti tonight. What do you say?'

'All right.' Renata tried to smile. 'Your tolerance is amazing, Karen. I'm deadly company these days and still you put up with me.'

'Forget it! We all have bad times and sad times. I've seen what these last weeks have done to you, and all because you're so tragically well acquainted with—the game, as you so quaintly call it. No one should have to go through that even once, and from what you told me, Grant Fowler understood that too.'

Yes, Renata thought. He had understood, so he wouldn't contact her on his return to Kathmandu. He would go out of her life and perhaps forget her, but would she ever be able to rid her heart of his presence and do her own forgetting?

The weeks of unremitting anxiety and tension had taken a cruel toll, as she realised, standing naked in front of her bathroom mirror later that night. The flesh had melted from her body, her limbs and even her face, making her cheekbones look even more prominent in contrast to the hollows beneath. Her skin had a horrible, unhealthily waxen pallor that emphasised the savage shadows of sleeplessness and even her hair looked lifeless, its silky sheen dulled, and only the suffering shape of her vulnerable mouth and the look in her eyes testified that what ailed her had emotional rather than physical origins.

A day came when the expedition team arrived back in Kathmandu, and that same evening there was a welcoming reception for them at the Embassy, at an early, cocktail, hour, since they were due to attend another function at the palace later. They would all be there, Renata learnt, with the exception of most of the Sherpas, who had returned to their homes in Sola Khumbu, and Pirie Jones who had flown out earlier from the airstrip just above Namche Bazar to get further treatment for his frostbite.

Renata was initially undecided about attending, knowing she could probably get out of it with few questions asked, but in the end she yielded to temptation, though she knew it was folly. She would just look in for a few minutes, she decided, between leaving her desk and going home—just to see how Grant looked. He knew he must leave her alone and anyway, knowing what she did of climbers, it was too soon for them to be able to react to life down off the mountain.

Oddly, though she had remembered the psychological effects, she had forgotten the physical changes that took place at high altitude, and she was momentarily shocked when she entered the reception room, her eyes swiftly locating the group.

There was a tendency to stick together, as if only their fellow climbers had any relevance for the moment, a residual manifestation of the dependence that would have developed on the mountain where their lives had depended on each other. Unnoticed, Renata stood watching them, those gaunt men, their beards not yet removed, who had climbed the highest mountain in the world and used up their last reserves of strength to do so, pushing their powers of endurance to the utmost limits and perhaps beyond.

Even the non-climbers, Leo Summers and Bill Thurlow, had shed enormous amounts of weight. It was normal, as Renata knew, and they would soon regain both strength and weight now that they were down, and yet for the first time ever she was shocked by the evidence of man's mortality.

Unable to tear her gaze away from Grant, she continued to stare at him, her heart slowly cracking as she realised anew things she had already known. He was a man, a human being. Down here, he had appeared almost as a god, his electric vitality unquenchable, but against a mountain even he was frail, as vulnerable as anyone. This time he had not been destroyed, but another time?

His glance swept over her and then returned briefly, and even at this distance Renata could see the empty expression, the blankness. He knew her, he recognised her, but he could not yet react to her, and she was relieved.

'Renata?' It was Ang Phurba who had extracted himself from the group and come across to her, perhaps slightly less wasted than the others because the heights were closer to his natural environment than to theirs and thus less of a shock to his constitution.

'Success, Ang Phurba.' She managed a smile. 'Well done, and congratulations.'

'Thank you, yes, being my first time on the summit.' He smiled and added, 'But not my last.'

She shook her head, still smiling, but wryly now, at the inevitability of it all.

'Are you the only Sherpa here?' she asked him. 'Where's Mingma?'

'Deciding to stay with his family in Namche Bazar. A holiday, you know. Lots of *chang*-drinking.'

'Of course,' she laughed.

His smile was shy. 'May I say? For the other Sahibs and Sherpas I make ceremony to dedicate my first time on the summit to God. To you, I will say the truth. By myself, I dedicate it to Ang Tsering Lama.'

Tears sparked in Renata's eyes and her mouth quivered as she leaned forward to kiss his brown cheek. 'Thank you for that.'

'He would be laughing, I think.'

'With joy, for you. He liked to laugh.' And she sighed for the absence of laughter in her own life.

'Yes, always laughing. I go back to the others now.'

'And I must go home.'

She was outside already when Grant caught up with her.

'Renata!'

She had frozen, staring helplessly at him, not knowing what to say, and he said nothing either. His eyes were no longer blank, but the expression in their dark grey depths was unreadable as they travelled over her face and figure right down to her slender legs encased in sheer taupe tights, the colour subtly repeated in the background of her flowered, soft wool dress.

'Grant, you were going to leave me alone.' Her voice had a desperate, gasping quality because pain was about to explode and she couldn't let it erupt in his presence. 'I need to know——'

'I'm not pregnant, that's all you need to know,' she said swiftly.

'You look terrible,' he said curtly, his eyes resting on her pale face.

'You don't look too hot yourself,' she retorted in a brittle tone. 'I must go. Congratulations, by the way.'

'Is that all you've got to say?' In front of her eyes, he was reverting to normal, casting off the Everest experience and adjusting to present realities. 'You kissed Ang Phurba, I noticed.'

'That was . . . different. There was a personal reason,' she said faintly, made suddenly breathless by the reviviscence of his old possessiveness.

'What?' he demanded.

'I said it was private. Don't ask me, and don't ask him either.'

He sighed. 'I can guess. I know you, Renata, and a man gets to know even someone as self-contained as Ang Phurba under the circumstances in which we've been living lately. My life has often been in his hands, and his in mine.'

'I must go,' she said again, nervously this time.

'Has nothing changed, then?' Grant asked harshly.

Eyes shadowed, Renata surveyed him, seeing the tautness of his bearded face and the darkly rebellious and possessive glow in his eyes. His time on the mountain, struggling against the elements, had perhaps hardened him, because his former understanding and acceptance were receding and she could see again the tendency to take over, to try and own her absolutely.

She knew then what she had to do, to make him free her.

Her voice as lightly dismissive as she could make it,

she said, 'Oh yes, things have changed. It worked, Grant, the thing I set out to do. Perhaps absence did it. I'm cured, you see. I've stopped loving you.'

Grant's mouth was a straight harsh line and his eyes smouldered angrily.

'We'll go into that later,' he stated tautly. 'Renata, there's something I have to tell you——'

'No!' she interrupted violently, her fragile composure snapping. 'There's nothing you have to tell me that I want to hear. Just keep away from me, Grant, stay out of my life!'

She swung away from him, and he stood watching her swift retreat for a while before sighing and going back into the Embassy building.

## CHAPTER EIGHT

AT EIGHT o'clock the following night Renata opened her flat door to find Grant standing there. His beard had been removed and he was wearing slacks, an open-necked shirt and carrying a lightweight jacket.

Momentarily, she experienced an overwhelming urge to step into his arms and be healed of all the loneliness and anxiety loving him had cost her. He looked so much more familiar now, with the beard gone, and so infinitely beloved.

Mastering the temptation, she said tartly, 'I thought I'd . . . freed myself yesterday evening. Grant, I asked you to stay out of my life.'

'I have to talk to you,' he said tersly, his eyes stormy, holding hers.

'I told you——'

'Renata, what I have to say has nothing to do with you and me,' he interrupted, moving into the hall and closing the door. 'Nothing to do with the situation between us.'

'What, then?'

'Can we sit down?' He was in the lounge already and she followed.

'Grant . . .'

'Sit down.'

Involuntarily she obeyed the note of command, sinking on to the couch, but Grant continued to stand in the centre of the room, looking down at her in brooding fashion, and she suddenly felt as if he was seeing through the Nepalese pants and pashima sweater into which she had changed on her return from work.

'Say whatever it is and go,' she said sharply, on the defensive as she felt her body begin to respond to the caress of his eyes.

Grant put down his jacket and took the single chair at right angles to the couch.

'Mingma told me you never wanted to know how your brother and Ang Tsering were killed, that you always refused to listen when he tried to tell you,' he began expressionlessly.

'No! I don't want to know!' Renata was agitated, her breath locking in her throat, her mouth twisting in anguish. 'If that's what you've come here to talk about ... I don't want to hear, Grant. Please! Just——'

'Listen to me, Renata,' he ordered sharply. 'You owe it to Ang Tsering and Darryl and to yourself to listen to what happened.'

She swallowed painfully. 'What ... why ... Did you find their bodies?' she choked.

Grant's face softened. 'No.'

'An axe, or something? Like they found Mallory's axe years afterwards?' Her eyes seemed to occupy most of her face now as she stared at him, riveted.

Pity for her flickered across his countenance. 'No, Renata, we found nothing. We were doing a different route, remember? I'm sorry. But I want you to listen to what Mingma told me.'

'I can't,' she gasped piteously. 'Please, Grant, don't make me, I can't bear it!'

'You must,' he said gently but inexorably. 'Perhaps it will even help you to get the whole subject of climbing in perspective. First of all, Mingma told me that initially your brother disliked your relationship with Ang Tsering?'

'Yes,' Renata agreed sadly, knowing that Grant would refuse to go away until she had heard him.

'Well, for a start, that prejudice vanished on the mountain. Mingma says Darryl came to have a great respect for Ang Tsering, a brilliant and courageous climber, and that a real friendship developed after a storm confined them to a snow-cave they'd built for a couple of days. They used to joke about how they were going to be brothers-in-law; they were the same age, of course, and the other members of the team took to calling them the terrible twins.'

A faint smile lit Renata's wan face now. 'I'm glad,' she confessed shakily. 'I loved Darryl and it used to hurt that he didn't think a Sherpa was good enough for me. But Grant, I don't want to hear any more.'

'It's all right, I'm not going to go into great detail about the accident,' he attempted to reassure her. 'Do you know what the western ridge of Everest is like?'

'Basically.'

'They had one of their camps on a very steep, narrow ledge, just short of sheer, the sort of place where you sleep with slings attaching you to pitons—if you sleep at all!' Grant paused, eyes looking beyond her as if he were recalling all the times he must have been in such situations, and Renata shuddered. He resumed, 'They were actually setting up the camp, Mingma says. There was some difficulty with one of the frames and Darryl freed himself to attend to it, and that was when he fell. They thought at first that he must have gone all the way, but then Ang Tsering spotted him caught on a minute outcrop way below. The others tried to dissuade him; it was highly dangerous, and pointless, to go down and risk killing himself when it was all too probable that Darryl was dead already, but he insisted that it wasn't such a great fall that there wasn't a chance he could be dying but not yet dead. He had to make sure and do what he could to ease him if he was still living.'

'Oh, God!' Renata breathed, appalled.

'They couldn't have attempted to restrain him physically in their situation. They'd all have fallen then, so they had to let him go.' Grant paused before finishing quickly, 'He went unroped so as not to imperil anyone else. He was half-way to where your brother was when a great portion of ice came away from the side, taking him and the shelf your brother was on with it.'

'Oh, God,' Renata repeated brokenly, lifting her hands to her face.

'Renata?' Grant said quietly, and she dropped her hands, curling them into fists on her lap as she looked at him questioningly. 'What it's important for you to know is what Mingma told me Ang Tsering said to him. He knew the risk he was taking, but he said he had to try because Darryl was your brother and you loved him and wouldn't want his last moments to be alone and in agony. Do you understand?'

'That . . . that——' She stopped abruptly, unable to go on.

'That there was a man to whom a woman meant more than anything else in the world.'

'But he died!' she protested in a cracked voice.

'Don't question the wisdom of what he did, Renata,' Grant advised. 'Just accept that he did it because he loved you. He was young and courageous and confident, and the situation didn't allow for quiet reflection, for weighing the cost to you of two deaths as opposed to one. He loved you, so he had to try.'

Renata was silent, absorbing it and gradually accepting it. Slowly she unclenched her fists, seeing the marks her nails had made. She looked up at Grant and he too was looking at her hands.

'Is gallant the word?' she asked quietly.

'I think so,' he confirmed.

'He had a . . . romantic spirit,' she added.

'Yes.'

'Thank you for telling me. I should have listened to Mingma, but perhaps I myself was too young four years ago to have accepted that . . . that young men . . .'

'That young men's hearts overrule their heads,' Grant supplied. 'He meant it for you, Renata.'

'I'm glad,' she said, standing up and adding prosaically, 'Would you like some coffee?'

'Yes, please,' he said mildly, staying where he was, and she was grateful that he understood her need to be alone for a few minutes.

In the kitchen, her thoughts stayed with the past for a while. She had said goodbye and let them go that day Grant had taken her into the foothills—her father, her brother and her sweetheart, as he had liked to call himself. Only her fear for Grant had called them up again in recent weeks, as examples of what could befall him. Their story was ended and she had accepted it, but the postscript was fitting and she was grateful for their brief resurrection.

*O Mane Padme Hum* . . . Silently she prayed them back to rest for the last time, two young men with whom she had shared part of her life. Her memory of them as people would be tenderly loving from now on; the horror of their deaths divorced from their personalities, but still the fate she would always fear for Grant for as long as she went on loving him.

Thus, it was Grant who filled her mind when she returned to the lounge with the coffee.

A silence fell between them which she didn't know how to fill. Grant was watching her unwaveringly, so she felt inhibited about looking at him as she longed to do, but she could still feel his intent, brooding gaze on her. She was acutely conscious of his presence, and of the dark mood that had fallen on him now. Her hand shook as she lifted the coffee cup to her mouth. Her nerves were taut, her stomach churning, and the memory of what had occured last time they had been here together slipped seductively into her mind. She began to tremble slightly, hoping desperately that he didn't notice, and she had difficulty in controlling her shallow, quickened breathing, while her body felt as if a deep, slow flush was stealing over it.

She still loved him, but she couldn't live with the long periods of fear his way of life would mean, and he didn't love her enough to eliminate that aspect so, somehow, she had to be free of him.

The tension between them had grown oppressive by the time she found the courage to look at him. She wanted to ask him to leave, but he spoke before she could.

'Why do you look so sick?' he asked abruptly.

'Why do you?' she retorted stupidly, putting down her cup.

'You know damn well that everyone loses weight at high altitude,' he said impatiently, his face tight and angry.

'Do you think I haven't been up Everest with you?' she flared bitterly, caution forgotten.

'Yes, I felt you there,' he returned sardonically. 'You haven't really stopped loving me, have you?'

'I have,' she protested, too quickly and too vehemently.

'I don't believe you.' Grant's voice was flat with denial.

'Why are you persecuting me?' Renata demanded desperately. 'I want you out of my life. You understood that, before you left, so why this, now?'

'Because I can't let you go.' He was on his feet now, moving purposefully towards her. 'You belong to me, Renata. You always will.'

'No!'

'Yes!'

Any further protest she might have made was silenced as Grant pulled her up into his arms. Renata's mind went blank and she was panting already at the first contact of their bodies, through the layers of their clothing, the long weeks of tension unleashed in immediate, explosive arousal.

Frustration made their need savage. Between long, fierce kisses they tore frantically at each other's clothes until they were both naked, falling on each other in an agony of hunger. There was no transfer to the bedroom this time. Grant was making love to her right there on the couch amid the softness of the tumbled pashmina shawls that had covered it.

'Ah, God, I've wanted this,' he groaned, his fingers kneading her swollen breasts. 'You came between me and the mountain. I kept thinking of you, feeling your presence . . . It was as if you were there on every pitch with me, watching everything I did, checking every belay . . . You never left me.'

'No, I never did,' she moaned. 'That's why ——'

But his mouth was claiming hers again and when he transferred it to her aching breasts she was incapable of speaking, whimpering with pleasure as his tongue struck the tautness of one nipple and stroked sensuously round the dark puckered aureole.

She was mindless with passion and pleasure, and at the same time aching with a terrible need, her body twisting and turning in the anticipation of assuagement. Her hands moved down over his body, to darkness and power, and wasted as he was after his struggle with the mountain, Grant still possessed a strength and virility that both excited and terrified her.

His hands too were moving down her body, slithering over her sweat-dampened flesh, over her hips, her stomach and her thighs, one hand dipping between them, coming to the soft warm crevice there, and she pulsated under his touch, crying out hoarsely for fulfilment.

His mouth on her, his fingers working relentlessly, he was stoking her already intolerable desire, and a pressure was building within Renata, the need for release a madness that drove out all thought, a pounding rage of wanting.

'Please, Grant, please!' She was begging for relief, for mercy, her passion at a frenzied pitch as she clung to him, gasping and sobbing.

'You're mine, aren't you, Renata?' he challenged harshly, dragging laboured, shuddering breaths into his lungs, while his eyes devoured hers, searching for the truth, demanding it.

'Oh God, yes!' she confirmed tempestuously, writhing against him, seeking the easing she craved so wantonly. 'Grant, please, don't torture me. I can't wait.'

'I don't think I can either,' he muttered unevenly as his rough hard thighs moved between hers. 'Oh God, Renata!'

He drove into her receptive body with an urgency that made her gasp, and his hard, hoarse sigh mingled with the sound, while her moist, slippery flesh embraced the passage of his manhood. He thrust deeper, varying his rhythm for her maddened pleasure, his hands gripping her, and Renata jerked convulsively in his possession, her soft femininity clinging voluptuously to his hardness, throbbing about him as his movements quickened, becoming powerfully commanding when he abandoned all control and drove violently towards his own release.

It was a summit of another kind, found amid the fury of a storm of incredible intensity, a peak of shared ecstasy that they reached together, their breathing accelerated as they approached it. A shuddering cry was torn from Renata as her deep internal contractions spasmed outward to reach every part of her body. Even her mind was pierced by the brilliant light of true rapture, and at the same time she heard Grant utter a primitive, passionate cry of wild climactic pleasure as they clung to each other before falling from the heights to lie gasping in each other's arms.

A groan escaped Renata as sanity returned and she realised what she had done, compounding the folly of loving a man with whom she could never live.

Oh God, she thought feverishly, if only she didn't know so much about what mountains did to men, she could have lived with him in the bliss of ignorance, looking forward to his returns instead of fearing never to see him again.

'Renata darling, what is it?'

Grant's hand was caressing her hot damp face, smoothing her hair back from her temple, and she realised that tears were flowing over her face.

'Why?' she sobbed against his chest. 'Why did you do this? Why wouldn't you listen to me? I said I wanted you out of my life.'

'Oh God, not again!' he exclaimed harshly, arms tightening about her. 'Haven't I proved anything to you tonight?'

'Yes, that I'm a fool,' she confirmed bitterly.

'That you're mine,' he insisted. 'You even admitted it just now, just as you admitted you were there on the mountain with me in spirit ... That's loving, Renata, your own very special kind of loving, and I'm not about to turn my back on it. I know you want me out of your life, that you're unhappy and frightened just now, but I'm afraid I'm not sufficiently self-sacrificing to humour you. I need you too much, and I believe you need me. We belong together.'

'Grant, please!' Renata tried to free herself.

'No, I'm not letting you go,' he stated, steely-voiced. 'Not now, tonight, not ever. You give me so much, your love, your passion, and I won't let you withhold them.'

She was too distraught to dissemble. 'I ought to hate you for what you're doing to me, I wish I could ... But I can't!'

'Thank God,' Grant murmured softly.

'It's so difficult,' she added, a world of despair in her voice.

'I know, darling, I know.'

Humiliatingly, he sounded sorry for her. The hand stroking her hair was tender, the body alongside hers warm and strong, and Renata was weeping again, but quietly now.

Grant had drawn one of the pashmina shawls about her and he let her cry, simply holding her and stroking her, his comfort wordless. He continued to hold her after her tears had stopped, and Renata lay quietly in his arms for a long time, her mind oddly blank in contrast to her heart which was ablaze with pain.

Then, gradually, she felt her body beginning to respond to the closeness of his, felt too the quickening of his in answer to her arousal, and she knew that she had to escape now or it would be too late for ever.

She sat up, trying to draw away from him, and her voice was breathless and lacking in conviction as she said:

'Grant, please go now.'

Grant's smile was slow and sensual.

'Ah no, Renata, I'm not letting you send me away this time. I'm staying with you tonight . . . and all the other nights.'

He stood, lifting her and carrying her through to her bedroom.

Her bed felt cold to begin with, but soon a deep burning flush was spreading over her entire body. He was utterly dominant, subduing her few protests with the commanding mastery of his hands and mouth and body, ravishing her until she lay whimpering and moaning beneath him. He demanded everything and denied her nothing, forcing from her those choked cries that pleaded for his possession.

Only then, when desire was rampant and irresistible,

did he take her, with a violence strangely blended with a piercing sweetness, and at the moment of penetration, Renata knew finally that he was absolute master in their relationship and she could only yield to his command. She was his to do with as he wished, to hold or to let go, to be summoned or dismissed.

When the long tremors racking her had subsided, she felt herself drifting naturally into sleep for the first time in weeks, vaguely aware of Grant's hold on her slackening as sleep hit him even before it laid a more gentle claim on her, and her last thought seemed inconsequential—he probably needed lots of sleep to repair the ravages of the mountain.

The mountain . . .

It had prevented or interrupted sleep for weeks past, and tonight was no exception, sated as she was and exhausted by emotion.

This time it was the most frequent of her dreams, that which she had come to think of as the Ice Fall dream, in which she watched a climber passing beneath a giant serac which, somehow, she knew she was going to topple and crush him. She also always knew that the man was Grant, although his protective clothing obscured him. Then there would come a point in the dream at which she would realise that she too was a climber, roped to him, as he led through the Ice Fall, her terror growing as he seemed to spend an eternity beneath that serac, moving in slow motion. Joined thus, they were as one and inseparable, and she knew that if he was killed, she too would die, and yet her fear was for him.

The serac was falling and belatedly she was trying to warn him, but she had no voice, her throat locked, and nor could she move because somehow her boots had become leaden and her crampons were inextricably embedded in the icy surface on which she stood.

Then suddenly as the rope jerked and tightened and she went blind, she found her voice.

Her own scream woke her, but she didn't realise it at first, struggling against the duvet and the hard warm hands that held her, thrashing about as she strove to free herself.

'No, no, oh no!' she was sobbing, shaking violently.

'Renata, wake up!' Grant's voice, sharp and authoritative, penetrated the miasma of terror that enveloped her. 'Renata, stop it!'

She opened her eyes. The bedside lamp was on and she was sitting up, her face wet with tears, while Grant held her firmly, having stopped shaking her when he realised she was awake. Renata stared at him in shocked disbelief.

'You're here,' she said stupidly.

'God, what was it?' Grant demanded shakily, his face pale, his eyes dark with shock. 'You were screaming. I've never heard anyone scream in their sleep before.'

'I had to wake up,' she explained dazedly, glad that for once there were arms to enfold her in these first shaken minutes after the dream. She was disorientated, her heart still racing, and fear continued to cling to her.

'A nightmare? You said my name when you first started thrashing about.'

His eyes were questioning, his hands gentle and comforting, but there was a note of reproach in his voice, as if he objected to having a place in her nightmares.

'You were in the Ice Fall . . . leading,' she endeavoured to enlighten him, although she knew she was probably making little sense.

'Ah, I see.' He sighed. 'It was hard work too, forcing the route, and it had changed by the time we came down. But I'm here now, darling.'

'It's always the same, the Ice Fall dream,' she went on with a weary sob. 'The others change, the falling ones, but not the Ice Fall one.'

Grant had stiffened at her first words and now he drew back a little, his gaze searching her white face and seeing the residual terror that lingered in her eyes.

'What do you——' He broke off and Renata could sense his sudden distress. 'How often do you have these dreams, Renata?'

Embarrassed now, she averted her face, muttering, 'Every night . . . I think.'

'Since when?' he demanded curtly.

'Since . . . I'm not sure. I think since you left Kathmandu. I don't know . . . I suppose it's because I think about it all day and then, at night . . . I get so frightened, Grant,' she concluded despairingly.

'Yes, you know too much about it all, don't you?'

To her surprise, the hand stroking down the length of her spine had begun to tremble.

'What is it?' she asked, looking up into his face again and finding it even paler than before.

He stared back at her for a few seconds, his mouth twisting, and the expression in his eyes was one she had never seen before. It was like looking into a dark hell of disturbance, and it frightened her.

'Grant?' she questioned nervously.

'It's all right,' he reassured her tightly as he pushed her gently back against the pillows. He got out of bed and turned to settle the duvet about her, completely unselfconscious about his nakedness. 'I'm going to get you

something to drink. What do you want? You really ought
to have something that will knock you out until morning.'

'I haven't got anything like that.' She lay looking at his
dark lean body, loving it, the last remnants of nightmare
dispersing as she remembered how he had joined himself
to her that last time, with such sweet savagery.

'No Scotch? No pills either, I suppose?'

'Nothing.' She gave him a shy smile. 'Tea. I'd like
some tea.'

He grimaced. 'All right, I won't be long.'

'Aren't you cold?' she asked stupidly before realising
that he knew what real cold was and that it was
something Kathmandu never experienced.

But he only asked absently, 'Where are my clothes?'

Renata smiled faintly. 'In the lounge. Remember?'

The smile of acknowledgement he gave her before
leaving the bedroom was forced, and she was perplexed.
Could he really be offended because she had dreamed of
him and the mountain? But then why was he trying to be
kind, looking after her, making tea?

She gave it up and relaxed against the pillows, rather
liking the feeling of being cared for. She had finally
accepted that Grant must dictate her life, and she
supposed there would be these moments of warm
contentment at times, as well as the carnal hours of rich
passion when the incandescent attraction between them
found physical expression in their erotic lovemaking.

And for the rest . . . terror; but apparently Grant no
longer sympathised with that, but expected her to control
it—endure it. She would try, she thought. She would have
to learn to keep it to herself, as her mother had done, and
not bother him with it. But she did wonder how long even
someone mentally and emotionally stronger than she was

could continue living like that, perpetually attended by
fear, with not even the hours of sleep truly free of it,
without cracking up in some way.

As he had observed, she knew too much about it all,
the risks entailed, and it was that knowledge that was
driving her rapidly towards breaking point. Grant and
every other climber and their women would probably
despise her if she had a nervous breakdown. They were
strong, they could take it—as she had once been able to
but no longer could.

Grant was wearing his trousers when he returned to
the bedroom with a tray, but he was barefoot and hadn't
bothered to put his shirt on.

He was treating her like an invalid, Renata realised as
he re-settled the pillows for her so that she could sit up,
poured milk into her tea and offered her sugar. Then he
sat down on the edge of the bed, facing her, and picked
up the mug he had brought for himself.

'What's that you're drinking?' she asked.

He looked rueful. 'Coffee. I still can't face tea or soup
or any of the revolting brews we lived on on Everest.'

'I'm sorry there isn't any proper drink in the flat,' she
apologised.

'Meaning alcohol? That's something that's never done
me either any harm or good,' he told her lightly. 'I've
never known whether to consider myself fortunate or the
reverse. It depends on one's mood and what one wants
from drinking, I suppose.'

'Yes. Karen—my friend from the U.S Embassy—said
she saw you one night in Sola Khumbu village when you
were on your way out to Everest.' Renata smiled.
'According to her, you were knocking back vast

quantities of *chang* and then walked out as sober as when you'd started.'

'I remember that night,' he agreed ironically. 'It was one of the occasions when I've considered my immunity definitely unfortunate. I thought it would help if I could get a bit drunk.'

Renata sipped her tea and looked at him.

Grant's smile had a dry quality. 'Yes, you know why.'

'I'm sorry,' she said softly.

A silence fell and she wondered a little at the brief exchange that had just taken place. It was as if they had been making conversation simply and solely in order to fill up a silence, and she had sensed the element of constraint with which Grant responded to her.

Now they had run out of words and the silence between them became extended. There was a tension too, and this time it emanated from Grant, she realised.

He replaced his mug on the tray and sighed, saying, 'And God knows what will help in the future.'

'What?' Renata was too disconcerted to be polite.

His mouth had a bitter curve as he looked at her.

'You win, Renata,' he said reluctantly.

'Grant . . .'

'You've asked me often enough,' he went on. 'Now I'm complying. I'll stay out of your life from now on.'

'But——'

'I never realised, you see.' Suddenly he sounded infinitely weary. 'I never realised how bad it was for you . . . that it was constantly in your mind and even with you in sleep. It's making you ill, isn't it. It would destroy you eventually—it's destroying you already—and I just can't handle that sort of responsibility.'

Renata's sapphire eyes were dark with incomprehension. 'But you said——Why now, Grant? Why have you changed your mind?'

'You should have heard yourself screaming! There was sheer, mind-breaking terror in the sound.' Grant's voice had sunk almost to a whisper, the sound appalled, and yet, as Renata looked into his eyes, she saw the gathering of resentment. 'God, I must have seemed an insensitive bastard, not to understand. It's a miracle that you don't hate me yet ... Renata, I want you to know that I did actually understand before I left Kathmandu. I accepted that I had to get out of your life; I realised when I discovered who you were that you wouldn't be able to handle a relationship with me. Then—I don't know. On the mountain, I kept thinking of you. Perhaps you know how it is from your father and the others. At night, I'd be there, cold and cramped in a box-tent, wondering what sort of crazy masochist I was to let myself in for so much strain and sheer physical discomfort, and I'd promise myself all the good things in life if I could only get off there—warmth, and space, and ... you. Tonight, I was still in that frame of mind to a degree. What I wanted was all that mattered, and to hell with your wishes. I'm sorry now, believe me, more sorry than I can say. To hear you screaming like that, and realise it was something you went through every night ... I can't——' He broke off momentarily, giving her a strangely hunted look. 'I can't do that to you. Do you understand? You're free, Renata.'

# CHAPTER NINE

STARING at Grant, Renata felt hysterical laughter bubbling up within her, but she suppressed it.

She had to face it, once and for all. He didn't love her. He certainly didn't love her enough to even consider academically the question of giving up climbing. The idea had never crossed his mind, and since he didn't truly love her, there was little purpose in her bringing it to his attention.

Anyway, she knew climbers. To stay away from the high places would be a living death, and she loved Grant too much to want that for him, even if he could have offered such a sacrifice.

She had no choice but to accept his decision to leave her life, and it was what she had wanted all along, wasn't it?

Grant's face wore a dark, introspective look as he took the cup she handed to him and replaced it on the tray, and Renata's heart twisted painfully with love and compassion. He might not love her, but his desire for her was something consuming, rare and special.

She said softly, 'I'm sorry, Grant. It would have worked if I wasn't such a coward.'

'It's not mere cowardice when it lies even in your subconscious and you have terrifying nightmares all the time,' Grant returned harshly. 'Don't apologise for something you can't help, Renata. God knows, your history makes it understandable, and inevitable. You know too much, and you've lost too much.'

'Yes.' She sighed, wishing she was without that knowledge, that she could cut out the memories that made her fear for him, and accept his compulsion to climb philosphically.

He hesitated before saying, 'How much damage have I done, Renata? Can it be mended?'

'I don't know,' she answered honestly, touching his hand where it lay on the duvet, sensing that he was the one in need of comforting at this moment.

'Can you stop loving me?' he added. 'Can I make you? God, you ought to hate me now, and I wish you did. No I don't! But it would be easier for you then, wouldn't it? But to make you hate me, I'd have to hurt or humiliate you, and I can't do that to you.'

'You only have the power to hurt me because I love you,' she told him gently. 'No, Grant, I don't think I'll ever be able to hate you. As for stopping loving you . . . that's something for time to do, if it can.'

'Time, and absence,' Grant agreed. 'I suppose I ought to leave you. I'll finish dressing in the lounge and let myself out.'

Renata was still touching his hand, holding it, and her grasp tightened now. On an impulse born of love, her other hand pulled down the duvet and she lifted his hand, laying it on the softness of her breast, and feeling her loins grow instantly heated in response to his touch.

'Grant . . . Till the morning?'

She was still shy, not knowing how to ask him.

'The last time, Renata?' There was a stifled groan just audible. 'For goodbye? God, I don't think I can bear it!'

But already his fingers were working urgently at the tautening satiny flesh, stroking the tender nipple until it grew hard and swollen, hot beneath his fingertips, and he wasn't proof against the slim pair of arms that came up to encircle his neck, drawing him down to her.

Swiftly they were lost in a torrid welter of sensuality. Renata waited impatiently as he eased his trousers from his aroused body, reaching for him, and their lovemaking assumed a quality of desperation now, each of them knowing it would be for the last time.

Her kisses and caresses made Grant gasp, and he pleasured her in return, each of them almost recklessly generous in satisfying the other, because this was all they would ever be able to give. Renata's mind and heart were filled with an agony that was in stark contrast to the rapture of her body. This was the last time her hands would stroke his body, the last time Grant's mouth would madden her with those sensuous, suckling kisses at her breasts, the last time . . .

But if she lived with him every time would feel like the last time.

Then all thought faded as she felt his mouth on her so intimately that she gave a small cry, his tongue caressing her very tenderest flesh.

He moved up over her again, the weight of his body along the length of hers, hair-roughened chest crushing her breasts, flat hips against the female curve of hers, the darkness at the base of their bodies merging, thighs throbbing together.

'I love you,' she sighed as his mouth descended to hers and she was opening to him, arching, thighs and knees clamped to him like a vice, and they both groaned with mingled pain and pleasure as he entered her, making them one.

Renata's eyes shut as her melting femininity yielded

and closed on the hard flesh, and her mouth pulsed beneath his, his tongue repeating the rhythm of his possession. Together they came again to their towering summit at the climax of their mutual ecstasy, and Renata heard Grant call her name with a mixture of pleas re and savage despair at the end.

Because it was truly the end . . .

Once again sleep claimed her, even more swiftly than before, and this time no nightmare woke her and if she dreamed at all she couldn't remember it in the morning.

It was the sound of the flat door closing that woke her eventually, a very final sound somehow, and the place where he had lain in the bed was cold. Grant would not change his mind again, she thought.

It was light outside, but still early, and she lay with her thoughts for a while, her body still replete from Grant's lovemaking, content with its memories of the night they had shared, although a deep sadness was seeping through her mind and heart.

When she got up and put on a robe, she found herself reluctant to begin the practicalities of preparing for the day, showering, dressing, breakfasting. Instead, she wandered through the flat seeking evidences of Grant's presence last night, but there were few—just damp towels in the bathroom and the pashmina shawls from the lounge couch still strewn untidily as they had been after the first explosive outpouring of their passion last night. He had picked her clothes up and added them to the untidy heap, she noticed before going through to the kitchen where she saw that he must have made himself more coffee before departing.

She made some for herself and took it back to her

bedroom, pausing to pick up her discarded clothes in the lounge.

Sitting in bed once more, she discovered that she was shivering and not even the coffee could warm her. She felt empty and sad. She and Grant had parted for the last time. There was no longer any dilemma, no choice to be made. He had gone.

Last night had been an ending. Today ought to be a beginning, the beginning of learning to forget, but she knew now that she was never going to be able to do that.

The irony of it was bitter. It was Grant who couldn't live with her fear. She had no such choice. She had to live with it one way or another while he still lived, until it destroyed her.

He didn't want the responsibility of causing her to suffer, and he didn't love her enough to eliminate the cause of her fear. The knowledge hurt as nothing ever had before.

She heard a few days after their parting that Grant and the rest of his team had flown back to England. Now the days were even emptier, the lengthening nights the worst hell of all, filled with aching yearning, her body tormented by the memory of his, her mind still full of fear because she knew he meant to make a winter attempt on Lhotse.

Winter, the cruellest climbing season of all in the Himalaya. Only long after spring and autumn were official seasons had the Nepalese govenment decided to recognise a winter season, and on this they had imposed a strict time limit, although the savage weather conditions extended well outside both dates.

Renata felt as if she lived two separate lives now, as the year drew towards its end, the secret inner life that was governed by her love for Grant and consequently filled with fear and longing; and the outward everyday life that others observed. The latter proceeded as it had before the advent of Grant. There was the Embassy during the day and in her off-duty hours she still took walks about the city, alone or with Karen, and still encountered little Hamir in the old part of town and answered his one-word questions.

Also, as in the past, Renata and Karen hiked or cycled in Kathmandu Valley, treated themselves to the occasional meal at a restaurant or hotel, and partnered Wes Davies and Alec Lumley whenever they came down from Sola Khumbu. Wes's relationship with his Sherpani had progressed, so he suited Renata as a companion who made no demands on her, and she suited him equally well, apparently, as he seemed to sense that she expected nothing more of him than friendship, and he was too discreet to ask if her interest lay elsewhere or was simply non-existent.

Karen's friendship too was of inestimable value to Renata. With her there was no need to force smiles if she was feeling low because Karen knew she remained unhappy and was sympathetic, tactfully accepting Renata's disinclination to discuss Grant Fowler any further. She was unaware that Renata had had further contact with him after his return from Everest; that episode was too personal to be shared.

Renata had hoped, not very confidently, that perhaps by never talking about Grant and trying not to think of him, she might succeed in burying her love, just as she had once buried her anguish at the deaths of Ang Tsering Lama and her brother.

It didn't work, though. She never talked about him,

but she did think of him, constantly. She also found that she could no longer deliberately ignore the world of mountaineering. Instead, she was avid for news, not just from the Himalaya, but from the Karakoram, the Pamirs, the Hindu Kush—everywhere. Soon after Grant had left Nepal, a member of the Japanese expedition had died on Makalu, and the Australia-New Zealand expedition had suffered terrible hardship on Annapurna, a mountain even Stephen Armstrong had found coldly terrifying. Those events had depressed Renata for weeks, but still the compulsion to seek news continued. She couldn't help herself. Now, suddenly, she was aware of what was going on, who was climbing what, just as she had always been up until four years ago.

She knew when Grant returned to Nepal for his winter attempt on Lhotse. His team was the same as that for Everest save for the man who replaced Pirie Jones who was still having his frostbite treated in London. Ang Phurba went with them again, but the liaison officer and Sirdar were different men.

This time, Renata didn't make the mistake of attending any functions at which Grant was likely to be present, but she was aware of the team's movements, knowing the date of their departure from Kathmandu and when they arrived at the mountain. Once again, she was the prey of intense fear, nightly waking sweating and screaming, grateful for the fact that her flat was comparatively soundproof.

As with Everest, she was climbing Lhotse with them, losing weight along with sleep and appetite.

Still she made sporadic attempts to overcome her obsession, knowing it was destroying her. Grant would be spending Christmas on the mountain, and Renata made plans to be away from Nepal for the break in the hope that her concentration on Lhotse might be distracted.

Her circle was splitting up for the holiday: Wes had by now proposed to his Sherpani and was taking her home to Auckland to meet his family, Alec was heading for the delights of Bangkok, while Renata and Karen were travelling by train to Delhi.

It didn't help. Shopping for anklets and toe-rings in Chandani Chowk's Silver Street or strolling through Connaught Place in that lovely city with as many trees as people, Renata's thoughts remained with Grant on Lhotse.

She and Karen shared a hotel room in order to economise, and Renata was embarrassed when her scream awoke both herself and Karen and probably the people in the adjoining rooms after she dreamed that Grant was falling from a high place, hurtling through the air while in one of the quirky touches dreams so often contain the choughs soared about his plummeting body as she herself watched helplessly.

'God, Ren!' Karen was as shocked as Grant had been, sitting up and staring at her across the space between their beds after switching the light on. 'That must have been some nightmare!'

'I'm sorry. I should have warned you,' Renata muttered self-consciously, her heart still racing from the terror she had experienced. 'I suppose I hoped a change of scene, being away from Nepal, would alter the pattern.'

'Are you trying to tell me this is a regular occurrence?' Karen demanded incredulously.

'I'm afraid so,' Renata murmured shamefacedly.

'Since when?'

'Since . . . Grant.'

Karen swore, reflected a few seconds and asked, 'You still love him, then?'

'Yes.'

'Then you might as well let him back in your life and let him know what you're going through on his account, instead of suffering alone,' Karen said practically.

'He does know.'

'And he still wouldn't quit?'

'I didn't ask him and he didn't offer,' Renata informed her flatly. 'This time it was his decision to stay out of my life. I never told you, but I saw him . . . after Everest. He can't handle that sort of responsibility.'

Karen looked at her curiously. 'You know, babe, you make him sound a total bastard, but can he really be? You wouldn't love him if he was, or would you? Isn't it possible that he just doesn't want you to have to suffer and figures that if he's out of your life you'll . . . get over it, stop loving him?'

'Perhaps,' Renata conceded. 'I hoped the same thing originally, but it hasn't worked.'

'It's a bitch of a situation, isn't it?' Karen offered sympathetically. 'Is there no compromise solution you could work out?'

'I don't know. I don't think so.' Renata managed to produce a rueful smile. 'Tell me the truth, Karen! Apart from waking screaming, do I still seem normal, rational—sane?'

'I guess,' Karen allowed. 'You were always a quiet one, still waters run deep and all that, and you're even quieter now, and sort of pale and interesting. Sure, on the surface you're putting on a reasonable show, but that's all it is.

You can't go on like this. Shouldn't you see someone?'

'Who?'

'God, I don't know! A therapist or analyst or someone?'

'Karen, I know exactly what I'm afraid of and what has caused my fear, and it's hardly irrational,' Renata said, slightly caustic. 'What I need is someone who'll tell me how to stop loving Grant Fowler.'

Karen shook her head. 'I just don't know! I'm glad I gave up on love. Sex is simpler.'

'I've always known you had more brains than me,' Renata retorted with faint humour.

'Or less of a heart!'

'The heart you've got I'm grateful for. I'm sorry I woke you and sorry you've had to listen to me,' Renata apologised. 'Put the light off again if you like. One blessing—it's usually only one nightmare per night. But I think I'd better give up staying in hotels.'

Karen grinned. 'Well, now that we're awake, I feel like calling room service. I've got this craving for tandoori chicken, followed by something grossly rich and sweet and fattening. What do you say?'

'You'll be having nightmares too! But I'd like some tea.'

'You'll never sleep after that yourself, they make it so strong here,' Karen laughed, but picked up the phone and placed the order. Then she regarded Renata consideringly. 'Ren, I don't know if you know and whether I should tell you. Grant Fowler is on Lhotse. I read it in a newspaper.'

'Yes, I know,' Renata returned. 'I thought ... I thought coming down to Delhi might take my mind off it, but it hasn't.'

'What's Lhotse anyway? Is it dangerous? Sorry, all mountains are dangerous.'

Renata attempted a smile as she recited. 'It's the fourth highest mountain in the world, at 8511 metres, I think. It was the eighth of the fourteen eight-thousanders to be climbed—as with Dhaulagiri the Swiss were first. Reiss and Luchsinger.'

Karen was shaking her head again. 'And you say climbers are different! So are you, my friend,' she taunted gently. 'It's not everyone who can quote facts like that!'

Renata moved her head in acknowledgement. 'But it's nothing to do with Grant. It's the way I was brought up.'

'I'd say you were brought up to share your life with a man like Grant Fowler! Renata, if three men you loved hadn't died mountaineering, you'd be proud of him!'

'I am anyway,' Renata confessed ruefully. 'Karen, when he and Ang Phurba made it on Everest, I thought—they've still got to get down. But there was this little part of me that was thinking—my man did that. I loved him, and I was proud. But I'm also a coward. I know too much.'

And that would always be the case, she thought continually in the days that followed.

She and Karen did not stay long in Delhi and the long periods of train travel to and from the city used up a considerable amount of the short leave they had at their disposal.

Grant and his team were still on Lhotse when they returned to their respective Embassies in Kathmandu, but a few days later the Nepalese Ministry of Tourism announced a successful ascent by the pair of Grant Fowler and Ang Phurba, followed a few hours later by a semi-solo success by Pat Fiore. Conditions had been very hazardous and had deteriorated so rapidly that there would be no attempt to put anyone else on the summit. They were coming down, miraculously minus injury, illness and frostbite.

Renata tried to ignore all tidings of them after that, but somehow she was always aware of where Grant was. She knew the stages of his trek back to Kathmandu; she knew when he arrived in the capital city, literally able to feel that he was closer than he had been.

Still she kept away from all functions at which he and his team were likely to be present, strongly tempted to seek him out just once more but knowing that to do so would benefit neither of them. For both their sakes, she must keep away and get on with making what she could of her life. Reminders of what they had shared would do no good.

But she was unable to resist indulging in speculation about him, wondering how he thought of her these days, if he did so at all.

It was all too likely, she reflected as she strolled through the old part of Kathmandu with small Hamir at her side late one January afternoon, that Grant's recovery had been quicker than hers was proving to be. By now, another woman probably occupied his thoughts and shared his life when he was down off his mountains, someone who was either too strong or too unimaginative to burden him with her fears.

Renata's pale face wore a habitually closed expression, guarding the bleak anguish of her mood from unsympathetic eyes.

Why couldn't she have been stronger, able to accept Grant's way of life? She had lost him even before the

mountains took him and she wouldn't even be a happy
memory to him. If he thought of her at all these days, it
was probably as a neurotic he had been unfortunate
enough to desire for a while before turning again to the
type of woman who suited him better. He probably
counted her as the one disaster of his life and was glad to
be free of her.

He would have experienced none of the difficulties
confronting her now, none of the agony of trying to
forget, an impossible task when he filled her thoughts
almost exclusively and not even her sleeping hours were
free of him.

Renata glanced down at Hamir's dark head as he
strutted at her side, his inquisitive eyes darting ahead
and from side to side in search of some new sight to
educate his hungry mind. He was one of the few
distractions she knew these days. He was such a dear
little boy, at home in the streets of the old quarter of his
city and so bent on supplementing the education he was
receiving at school in this other school of life, his sturdy,
independent but still babyish figure clad in clean white
shirt, neat navy shorts, and socks and shoes a familiar
sight to his fellow citizens. Shopkeepers loved him, and
so did Renata. He often attached himself to her these
days, as if he sensed her sadness and was offering her the
only comfort he had to give, his company.

Renata thrust her cold hands into the pockets of the
reversible patchwork Nepalese jacket she wore with
jeans and soft boots. They were approaching the wide,
busy road that divided the old poor quarter, where the
only vehicles were generally bicycles, from the newer,
more affluent areas of Kathmandu.

It was also the line at which Hamir's freedom ended,

as his parents had forbidden him to cross the road, and Renata looked down to say goodbye to him, but Hamir's attention had been captured by the crowd of pedestrians who had just come across while the traffic light was green.

'Man,' he said, glancing up at her.

'What man?' Renata asked indulgently.

'Maybe your man.'

Her eyes followed the direction he had indicated with an expressive jerk of his head.

I'm falling apart, she thought wildly.

She was shaking so uncontrollably she thought she might fall to the ground, and her face was openly vulnerable and so spectrally pale that her anguished eyes looked like great inky pools in contrast.

Grant was only a few yards away and he had seen her by now. Ultra-lean after being on Lhotse, he still wore a look of deep fatigue. He stood absolutely immobile, staring at her; it was if they transfixed each other, with their eyes alone, because neither of them seemed capable of moving. Gradually, however, Renata became aware that his regard contained a growing anger that filled the dark grey eyes with a stormy turbulence and made them flash tempestuously, while his mouth hardened.

Why?

Renata couldn't understand what was happening to her. That dark, furiously accusing countenance filled all her vision, and her reaction was almost entirely physical. Her body and hands shook violently, her mouth was trembling and her heart was thudding at a painful, panic-stricken rate. She felt sick, faint and dizzy, and she only knew she couldn't yield to it here. She couldn't collapse in front of him.

She guessed why the sight of her had angered Grant. She knew what she must look like standing helplessly here on the edge of the pavement, trapped by his gaze, and it must be obvious to Grant that he was the cause. He had walked out of her life because he didn't want the burden of knowing he was responsible for what his way of life did to her nerves, and now he must be realising that his attempt to evade such a burden had been in vain.

Frantically, Renata knew she had to get away from here, get back to her flat and let it happen there—whatever it was that was making her shake so badly. Grant would be even more furious if he realised just how bad it was—if she came to pieces in front of him.

He would hate her!

Her only thought was to escape. She had forgotten everything else, including Hamir, who was staring at her curiously. All she was conscious of was the need to get out of Grant's sight, and that was imperative.

The urgency of the need finally gave movement to her shaking limbs, although they remained weak. She stepped off the pavement, and that was when the world exploded in a cacophony of sound.

'Watch, watch!' screamed Hamir and she thought she heard Grant calling her name at the same time as tyres shrieked excruciatingly and several other voices shouted.

I'm too late, she thought detachedly, because she was falling or flying or floating. A momentary numbness was succeeded by pain, and then more pain as a brief flight ended in an abrupt crash, after which her mind went mercifully black.

The Nepalese driver of the car had applied his brakes the moment she stepped into the road, but he was too close to avoid the knock which had sent her spinning into the shouting cyclist who had slowed as he realised what was happening but found himself trapped between the car on his right and the crowded pavement on his left. He and Renata went down amid a tangle of bicycle wheels from which he extracted himself, bruised, grazed and shocked, a few seconds later, but Renata continued to lie there at the side of the road while a crowd gathered round her oddly sprawled form.

Grant had been one of the first to reach her, removing the bicycle from where it lay across her legs, but when a young girl announced in Nepali that she was a nurse he moved back to give her room, sharply telling the crowd to do the same.

He assured himself that she was alive, but how bad her injuries were, he had no way of knowing. The shopkeeper who had sprinted back to his shop across the main road immediately after the accident returned to say that an ambulance was on its way. A traffic officer had arrived already, but Grant hardly heeded him, or the excited crowd which included the cyclist and the driver of the car, who were shakenly agreeing with each other that there was nothing they could have done to avoid hitting the girl.

He was vaguely conscious of someone small crying loudly beside him and tugging at his hand, and after a moment he turned and picked the little boy up in his arms because he felt utterly helpless and at least it was something he could do.

'Dead?' sobbed Hamir, clutching at his shirt.

'No, not dead,' Grant answered curtly, eyes following the little nurse's examination. 'But hurt.'

'Much blooding,' Hamir gulped. 'She is walking. I shout, but she is walking.'

'Yes, she just walked,' Grant sighed, his arms tightening about the child, the only other person here in all this crowd who knew Renata and was personally distressed by the accident.

He stared down at Renata. She looked so small lying there, a pathetic little heap, and the bright colours of her jacket were garish beside her white face and the blood that seeped from the side of her brow and oozed from her grazed and lacerated hands which had somehow come into contact with the bicycle spokes.

The anger he had felt on first seeing her was forgotten. He could only remember what had followed, those moments of sheer, unadulterated fear that had lanced through him as he realised she was going to be hit.

He had known fear before, on a variety of mountains, but never of such helpless, agonising intensity, and he hoped never to experience it again. A few fleeting moments of it had been to look at a darkness too appalling to contemplate; sustained, it could lead to madness.

Hamir was talking to him, but he didn't hear. He watched the nurse's small capable brown hands move exploratively down one side of Renata's inert body and went on thinking about fear.

Was that the sort of fear she knew, not just for a few moments at a time, but through all her waking hours and in the darkness of her dreams as well?

# CHAPTER TEN

RENATA couldn't decide if she was awake or dreaming. She knew she had fallen apart. That was why she had hurt so much earlier, when she had wanted to cry, but they—anonymous they with kind but firm brown hands—had stopped her, sending her back to the blackness before the tears had properly started.

Now she didn't hurt so much, but she felt uncomfortable, all wrong somehow, so they must have tried to put her back together again.

Like Humpty-Dumpty. But they had got it all wrong, or else parts of her had gone missing.

She said, or tried to tell them, it hadn't worked. She remembered the brown hands and knew she had to speak in Nepali or Sherpa, but she sounded so slurred that they couldn't possibly understand, and anyway the answer came in English, little more than a whisper.

'What is it, Renata?'

'Won't mend,' she tried again, relieved to know she could speak her own language.

'What won't mend?'

'Me.' She tried to open her eyes, but her head was starting to hurt now.

There was a pause and she could sense their distress at hearing the truth, but then the same voice said quietly, 'You'll be fine.'

She was in bed, of course, she realised, but it didn't feel

170

like her own bed. That made her force her eyelids to lift, though the pain and the light made her wince.

Grant was standing at the foot of the bed, his dark face blurred because she couldn't focus properly. Compunction pricked at Renata. He mustn't see her like this, now that she had fallen apart. He didn't want the responsibility. He had said so.

'Go away,' she said, but he didn't move and she grew agitated. 'Go away, Grant!'

She couldn't move, so he must be the one to go. Why couldn't he understand that? She tried to sit up, but she couldn't. Then a feminine voice spoke in Nepali and Renata saw Grant understand at last, moving away, and she felt resentful because he had listened to this other person but not to her.

There were no further illusions the next time she awoke. She remembered exactly what had happened, appalled at the possibility that her stupidity might have caused injury to others, and it took the Nepalese doctor and nurse a while to convince her that she was the only casualty.

'And Hamir?' she asked, ashamed. 'Poor baby, he must have got such a fright!'

'Who is Hamir?' Dr Ranawat asked.

'A little boy. He was there.'

'We have heard nothing of him. Perhaps Mr Fowler might know? You can ask him when he——'

'No!' Renata's eyes grew stricken. 'No, he mustn't see me again. I can't! I can't bear it. Tell——'

They pacified her, promising her she need have no visitors at all if she didn't want them.

'No, just not him ... Mr Fowler,' she told them

weakly, feeling a temptation to weep. 'Doctor, what's wrong with me?'

He listed her injuries, of which the most serious had been that to her head, although the most uncomfortable would turn out to be the massive bruising all down the right side of her body and leg, with muscle injuries to the arm, wrist, knee and ankle on the same side.

'One good side,' the nurse teased gently after he had gone. 'Left side, your clothes were torn but no injuries. Except your hands, of course.'

Renata was horrified by her hands when the dressings were changed, although she could see that the damage was superficial. Typically, while her more serious injury was soon no more than a small scar surrounded by grazing and not even needing a dressing, the hands took a long time to heal and still caused discomfort, not to mention inconvenience, even when her bodily bruising had become little more than a stiff ache. Her first full day in hospital, she tried to write to the motorist and cyclist, apologising for the carelessness that had involved them; it had taken her all afternoon and her nurse had found her in tears.

'I keep crying,' Renata muttered frustratedly. 'I'm not even thinking of anything and I suddenly find myself crying. Is that why I'm in a private ward?'

The nurse didn't know, and nor did the Ambassador's wife when she arrived during the evening visiting hour to see if there was anything she needed or anyone she wanted informed, but apparently it was not the Embassy's doing.

'Why are you not asleep yet?' a new doctor asked, doing a late round that night.

'I don't know.' Renata was embarrassed, afraid to sleep in case she woke screaming, and her fear seemed to counteract the mild sedative that had been administered earlier, since she was still wide awake.

'You are worried about something?' he questioned her after discussing what she had been given with the nurse and deciding to risk something extra.

'No . . . yes. Why do I keep crying?'

'That is normal after a shock, Miss Armstrong,' he told her. 'It will stop gradually, but this is why we want you to sleep, in order to build up the strength to assist your recovery.'

'Why am I in a private ward?'

'You didn't ask for it? You must speak to the doctor you saw first,' he told her. 'Dr Ranawat. He sent a message for you if you were awake. He has made enquiries about the child you were asking after—Hamir? Your friend Mr Fowler has been to see this child and reassured him that you will soon recover from your injuries.'

'Mr Fowler is a very famous man,' the night nurse said curiously when the doctor had left. 'He climbed Sagarmatha in the autumn, with Ang Phurba, another very famous man.'

The drug was beginning to take effect and Renata looked at her from beneath heavy lids. 'I didn't want him to feel responsible,' she murmured. 'But I'm glad he went to see Hamir. Was he here? Mr Fowler, I mean?'

'When you were still unconscious,' the nurse returned. 'Then you came round once and told him to go away. You wish to see him now? Tomorrow?'

'No. No, he mustn't see me,' Renata told her with an

effort, her speech growing slurred. 'Don't let him . . .'

'You sleep now.'

Renata did sleep, but she was unrested in the morning and slightly feverish. She knew she had had the usual dreams, although she couldn't remember them specifically, but the drug she had been given had denied her the relief of waking and she felt as if she had spent long hours in a bitter struggle to be free of the terror that had clutched her.

'I think something is worrying you,' her original doctor suggested in the morning. 'Your injuries are all coming along very nicely and you should be feeling much better this morning, instead of which—this! What troubles you?'

'Nothing.' Renata turned her head away to hide the tears filling her eyes. 'If my injuries aren't too bad . . . When can I go home?'

'Not just yet. Later, we will see.' He was non-committal.

'Then, please, can I ask you . . .' She hesitated, afraid of offending him. 'Please, I don't want any more drugs to make me sleep.'

'You feel they are responsible for the way you feel this morning?' He was interested.

'Yes.'

'Perhaps we will try something different, then.'

'I don't want anything different.'

'We will see if you fall asleep easily or not,' he conceded.

'Thank you.' She tried to smile at him, but it was a wobbly attempt. 'Dr Ranawat, can you tell me why I'm in a private ward?'

He immediately resumed his non-committal expression, murmuring, 'The request was made.'

Renata's lips trembled. 'Grant Fowler?'

'Yes.'

'I don't want him feeling responsible for me,' she said sharply.

'You are still reluctant to see him?'

'Yes. I don't have to, do I?' she asked nervously.

'Of course not——'

'And I want a transfer to a normal ward,' she added.

'That I fear I must deny,' said Dr Ranawat. 'It has nothing to do with Mr Fowler now. If you had made the progress I expected I would have agreed, but as it is . . . I am sorry.'

'Tomorrow, then? If I'm better tomorrow?'

'Then we will review the matter,' he promised.

Renata's depression deepened during the day. She hated herself for the way her eyes kept filling, but she felt too weak and exhausted to fight the tendency to weep. She had failed to free Grant of feeling responsible for her and he was probably angry, and resentful of her weakness in not getting over him.

Two colleagues from the Embassy visited her that afternoon, bringing some personal items that she had requested when the Ambassador's wife had visited her. Karen Richards came in the evening, having heard of the accident after trying to contact Renata at the Embassy, but Renata found she couldn't confide even in Karen.

'How did it happen?' demanded Karen.

'Oh, I stepped off a pavement without looking. It was my own fault,' Renata admitted dismissively before changing the subject. 'Look, the Ambassador sent me flowers. Impressive, aren't they?'

'Gorgeous. Ren, you really look terrible!' Karen refused to be distracted.

'You're supposed to cheer me up,' Renata reproached her teasingly.

'Sorry. Perhaps an enforced rest will do you good.'

Renata doubted it.

Finally, she pretended to be asleep when the nurse came, and later when the doctor's round was on, sheer tiredness had brought genuine sleep. She didn't know what time it was when she woke herself, crying out in terrible distress at the old Ice Fall dream, because almost instantly she felt the slight prick of the syringe needle that sent her back to a smothering oblivion from which she spent the rest of the night struggling to escape.

In the morning, Dr Ranawat drew a chair to the side of her bed, obviously meaning to spend some time with her.

'May I call you Renata?' he asked. 'You would have been Renata to all our nation, Nepalese and our Sherpa brothers, had Ang Tsering lived.'

'Grant Fowler again?' she asked flatly.

'Yes. I have just spoken to him by phone after reading the night staff's report. You should have told us about the dreams, Renata,' he went on. 'Then we would have known what to give you instead of experimenting and causing you to endure two very unpleasant nights.'

'I'm sorry.' Renata was desperately tired. 'I'm stupid as well as everything else. I used to be quite intelligent once—the brains of the family, my dad used to say.'

A faint smile lit the ascetic Nepalese features. 'You have had a long period of intense anxiety followed by the shock of your accident, and it is natural that you're now suffering from depression. It is not unusual, but I'd like to ask one of my colleagues to visit you this afternoon.'

'I can guess what sort of colleague,' Renata sighed wryly, thinking that Karen would approve. 'All right, you win.'

'Good. She is better qualified than I to recommend something that will allow you to sleep without fear tonight,' Dr Ranawats told her as he stood up.

'What's her name?'

He smiled. 'Also Dr Ranawat. She is my wife.'

Later in the morning, a nurse told Renata she could expect the lady Dr Ranawat at three. Renata lay lethargically in her bed, waiting for her, wondering idly if a woman was preferable to a man; would she be sympathetic or secretly despise her for her weakness? It didn't really matter. Either way, she would be very professional, and Renata now accepted that something had to be done. She couldn't go on like this.

But what I really need is a little happiness, she thought, staring at the ceiling, wishing her eyes would stop filling with these ridiculous tears. But Dr Ranawat wouldn't bring happiness, just counsel that she would have to do her best to follow.

She heard the sound of the door opening and closing, and tried to blink away the tears before looking at the doctor.

Only it was Grant Fowler who stood looking down at her, his face taut with some kind of strain.

'You must go away,' she whispered after a stunned moment. 'I've got an appointment, a doctor is coming to talk to me.'

'I know. I persuaded the Ranawat that you need me

more than you do them.' Grant's mouth twisted. 'Renata, I know you haven't wanted to see me, but——'

'I was supposed to stop needing you, so that I could stop being afraid,' she recalled bleakly. 'That's why I didn't want you to see me, because you'd know that . . . that it hasn't worked. I'm sorry, Grant, but you don't have to feel responsible. It wasn't your fault——'

'For God's sake, stop it, Renata!' he pleaded urgently. 'You make me feel so ashamed.'

'I don't want you to. That's why I didn't want——' She stopped as humiliation began to hit her. 'That's why you're here now, isn't it? Because you feel responsible . . . guilty——'

'I'm here because I love you!' Grant said the words unevenly, as if he fought with some emotion that threatened his self-control. 'I've loved you since . . . since the beginning, and I can't stop. I've tried, but nothing works.'

Renata's mouth shook. 'You've never said that before. Nothing works for me either.'

'I know.' He paused, then drew up the chair in which Dr Ranawat had sat that morning. 'I knew, because I could feel you with me on Lhotse even though I'd heard you were in Delhi, and then when I saw you, just before that car hit you . . . I hated myself then.'

'You were angry,' she whispered.

He was sitting now, but he wasn't relaxed. His eyes burned in his face, dark and intense.

'With myself,' he said. 'With my stupidity.'

She lay looking at him, with no lightening of her spirits, no warmth in her heart, only a deep, unending pain that was for both of them. Somehow she knew he was speaking the truth, that guilt had little or nothing to do with it. He did love her, in his way, but he would still climb his mountains.

She moved the bandaged hand that lay closest to him, wanting him to touch it.

'Grant, I'm sorry, so sorry,' she said shakily.

'Stop apologising, damn it,' he snapped. 'It's me!'

'It's both of us,' she said sadly.

He sighed and took her hand very carefully, as if he were afraid of hurting her.

'Your poor hands!' He looked up at her face, agony in his eyes. 'Oh God, Renata, if I've nearly succeeded in destroying you, I've done the same to myself! I've missed you, I've wanted you . . . I can't tell you! I thought I was going mad . . . I couldn't free myself. You haunted me, and I hated the thought that you might have stopped loving me, even though I hoped for your sake that you would stop. Only when I was on Lhotse did I know you hadn't, because I felt you with me again.'

'Grant.' Renata's voice was choked. She couldn't bear his distress, but she didn't know what to say to disperse it.

'And now I'm making you cry,' he added with bitter self-loathing. 'I just can't understand why you don't hate me!'

'I can't,' she told him on a note of despair, and a tear trickled from the corner of one eye and ran back into her hair. 'I love you.'

'And oh, God, I love you!' he exclaimed with odd violence. 'More than anything, more than life! Renata, can you forgive me? And marry me? Please.'

She was silent, swallowing painfully and looking away

from him. He had shifted his chair even closer to the bed and now he dropped his face to the hand he held. Only her thumb and the soft mound of flesh at its base were unbandaged, and Renata shivered as she felt his warm mouth there, lips caressing almost tentatively, his tongue stroking. Warmth was unfurling in her body, spreading outward, and a little gasp escaped her as Grant sucked gently at the soft flesh.

'Grant?' Her voice was barely audible and he looked up at her, his expression tense as he awaited her answer. 'Grant, for myself I would want that now; it would be preferable to the way I've been living these last few months, without you ... I've wanted you so badly. I would want that, except for what I know it would do to you. You'd be seeing me, constantly aware of how frightened I was ... I'm not brave enough to hide it. You'd feel ... guilty, wouldn't you? And then resentful because the guilt would spoil it for you, and finally you'd despise me for being a coward. I couldn't bear that.'

'I wouldn't be climbing,' Grant said quietly.

Renata stared at him uncomprehendingly and a purely nervous little gasp of laughter escaped her. 'What? You didn't ... I didn't——You did say that!'

Grant's smile was savagely ironical. 'You've been waiting a long time, haven't you? Why did you never ask me, Renata?'

'How could I?' Still she could hardly believe she had heard him say those words. A betrayal of himself, a sacrifice of unbelievable magnitude to her. 'I didn't expect ... I couldn't. You're a mountaineer.'

'You're a true Armstrong, aren't you?' He laughed

faintly. 'Renata, you haven't answered me. I want us to be married.'

'But . . . Grant, I can't—— You can't! You feel sorry for me——'

'Oh God, do you want the whole shameful story?' he demanded anguishedly. 'It's not pity, Renata, it's . . . the way I love you. This is why I'm so ashamed. I've known, since before I went to Everest, that all I had to do was stop climbing. I wanted to, I was tempted to, but— forgive me, I had this insane, arrogant idea that I'd be diminishing myself in some way if I did, that I'd be less than a man and lose my self-respect because it would give you too much power over me. I often thought about it, considered the possibility, but it seemed shameful to give up something I like doing for a woman . . . In fact, it was shameful to continue climbing, and stupid, selfish and self-destructive. I've harmed myself probably as much as I have you, Renata, by fighting so long, resisting the obvious. In one way, I realised how cruel I was being to both of us, but it only hit me fully the other day, when I saw you step in front of that car. I've never experienced a moment of pure fear like that before, fear of losing you, of your death . . . Oh, I'm explaining myself so badly! Can I just say that I love you and I'd rather live with you than die on a mountain—and I'd rather have you live with me than die under the wheels of a car. I don't want fear for either of us, not you, not me. It's not pity, it's love . . . the most important thing in the world—the only important thing in the world.'

Renata looked at his set face and smiled through her tears. 'I want to hold you,' she said shakily.

He moved, coming up close against her where she lay,

until she could fold her arms across his shoulders. His head was a sweet weight against her shoulder and breasts, his face buried against her softness, and she could feel him rigid and shaking as she clumsily stroked his dark head with one bandaged hand.

'I'm sorry I was so obstinate for so long.' His voice was muffled. 'I used to think it would feel like a defeat if I yielded . . . But it doesn't! It feels like a victory if you'll only accept it, darling.'

She went on smiling and stroking his hair, feeling the tension leave him gradually, until he shuddered, sighed and relaxed against her. Brought up among men who worshipped action, she was only now realising fully, as perhaps Grant too was doing, that it was more manly to love truly than it was to climb mountains. Real men weren't afraid to love. Grant was no longer afraid to love. Love was strength, not weakness.

But she said, 'Grant, dear Grant, I love you and I'll live with you and marry you, but how can I accept this? How can I return it? By promising never to cross another road?'

'You could try promising to look first,' he retorted.

'I promise,' she answered promptly. 'Grant listen to me and then decide. You don't have to do this . . . When you said you wouldn't be climbing any more, it was like . . . Oh, just to hear it and know you really meant it was enough, a miracle. Now I look to the future and I wonder if one day you won't regret it——'

'I love you!'

'Even loving me. One day perhaps you'll start looking to the mountains and . . . and regretting what you sacrificed, and resenting me.'

'Never that, Renata.' He looked up and his eyes were warm and tender. 'I never want to leave you again, so no climbing.'

'Grant, it doesn't matter. Climb if you want to. I'll still marry you, and I'll try not to . . . to——'

'Renata!' She saw him swallow emotionally. 'You're just too bloody generous! I don't deserve it and I won't accept it. Don't you understand? It's not important to me any more—you are! It was a compulsion, but you're an obsession and my love. I can live without it and not miss it, because I'll have something so much more worth having, and above all things, I want you to be happy and unafraid.'

'Are you sure?' She was still uncertain.

'God, yes! In a way it makes my obstinacy even more shameful because I've always known I could live without it. I used to wonder how I'd react if I ever got really bad frostbite resulting in severe amputation and I couldn't climb, and I knew I could live with it, without bitterness. That way, though, I'd have been forced to make a sacrifice. This way it's my own choice and finally a pleasure to make.'

'Yes, well, I suppose I'm preferable to frostbite.' Renata used her free thumb to caress his mouth. 'Grant, can we compromise, please?'

'No.'

'We must. I can't let you give it up completely. You once said I wouldn't be myself without my past. You wouldn't be who you are, the man you are, if you weren't a mountaineer. It's part of you. I need time with you, free of fear, but after that I want you to promise me that if ever you feel the need to go high again, you'll tell me, discuss it with me, and not just silently resent me because you had to give it up.'

'I promise,' he said abruptly, before smiling. 'But I'm not really doing this for you. It's for me.'

'Yes, and I accept it for now, but if ever it starts feeling like a sacrifice . . . Please? Then you must climb. I don't want sacrifices.'

'I can't imagine ever looking at it that way, but . . . We'll see.' Grant assured her. 'Renata, your father would be proud of you. I'm proud of you.'

'And I . . . Oh, Grant, I can't tell you how I feel,' Renata said fervently, her eyes alight with joy, her face suddenly transfigured into true beauty. 'I love you and for as long as we've got, I . . . I . . . Grant, would you kiss me? Please? I've been so lonely for you, wanting you.'

'Won't I hurt you?'

'I don't think so.'

He leaned over as carefully as if he feared she might break, and his mouth when it touched hers had a gentleness she had never known before. Renata felt tears sting her eyes as her heart swelled with love and pride.

'Oh God, Renata!' They were both shaking as the long healing kiss came to an end. 'Forgive me, forgive me for all I've done, for taking so long to know that it was you and only you I wanted. I love you and we'll never be apart again. No nightmares tonight, darling,'

'Never again, I hope,' she told him, her eyes luminous as he stroked her face with slightly trembling fingers.

'I'll stay with you anyway,' he decided.

'They won't let you.'

'They will.'

And they did. That night, as Renata's eyes closed for

sleep, their last sight was of the man who sat beside her bed, watching her with such love and adoration that she felt humbled, wondering why she should be so blessed with this chance of perfect happiness and vowing that Grant would never regret his choice.

She slept undrugged but dreamlessly, and when she woke in the early winter dawn he was still there. He was asleep, but he hadn't moved to a more comfortable seat. Instead, his head rested on his arm on the bed, and his hand was warm as it clasped her wrist above the bandaged hand as if he both sought and gave reassurance. Somehow she knew that hand had never left her all through the night, and her smile was tender. Soon they would sleep more comfortably.

Two weeks later, as Grant and Renata wandered through the old part of Kathmandu, a small figure appeared in front of them.

'Better?' demanded Hamir.

'All better,' Renata assured him, her face radiant.

'Happy?' he asked next.

'Can't you see?' she laughed, curving an arm through Grant's.

'Marry?'

'Yes,' Grant and Renata both said together.

Hamir gazed up at Grant. 'Sagarmatha?'

Grant laughed. 'No, no more Sagarmatha.'

'Very good,' Hamir approved, beaming.

Renata's eyes were alight with love as they moved on. Grant was living with her until she could leave her job when they would return to England and be married. Last night was the first time they had made love since her discharge from hospital, and it had been the most magical and deeply sensual experience of her life. To begin with, Grant had touched her as if she was something infinitely fragile, almost reverently, worshipping her with his hands and mouth and body, until he had realised that her love and need matched his. Then their desire had exploded in brilliant, matchless rapture as they soared together to their shared summit of ecstasy, and it was dawn before their passion was spent.

'You really and truly meant it, didn't you?' Renata said wonderingly.

'Did you doubt it?' His smile was like a caress.

'It still seems so . . . so miraculous!' she exclaimed with a touch of incredulity.

'Why?' Grant teased before his glance grew serious. 'There's no mountain in the world that is more beautiful or more beloved than you, no challenge more exciting than that of loving you, and no achievement higher than that of making you happy. I will make you happy, Renata.'

'You have already,' she answered him, her voice barely above a whisper as she was shaken by a surge of emotion. 'Grant, darling Grant . . . Can I make you as happy?'

'What do you think you're doing right now?' he retorted. 'When you look at me like that and I know that soon you'll be my wife, and sooner still you'll be in my arms . . . What's wrong with now? Let's go back to the flat!'

He was the urgent, stormy-eyed lover of last night again, and Renata was smiling as they turned to go back the way they had come.

Sometimes loving meant letting go, she knew, and it

might be that some day in the future she would be called upon to do just that, should Grant feel the compulsion to climb again, and by then she hoped she would be equal to the sacrifice.

But for now, he was hers as completely as she belonged to him, and there was a chance that he always would be, when love was such a unique power.

It was really up to her, Renata realised.

**ROMANCE**

# Variety is the
# spice of romance

Each month, Mills & Boon publish new
romances. New stories about people falling in
love. A world of variety in romance — from the
best writers in the romantic world. Choose from
these titles in May.

**THE SHADOW OF MOONLIGHT** Lindsay Armstrong
**DREAM OF LOVE** Kay Clifford
**SINGLE COMBAT** Sandra Field
**FANTASY UNLIMITED** Claire Harrison
**THE EAGLE AND THE SUN** Dana James
**A SAVAGE ADORATION** Penny Jordan
**CIRCLE OF FATE** Charlotte Lamb
**HAY FEVER** Mary Lyons
**TOUCH AND GO** Elizabeth Oldfield
**BROKEN SILENCE** Kate Walker
**\*A DANGEROUS PASSION** Jayne Bauling
**\*NO STRINGS ATTACHED** Annabel Murray

On sale where you buy paperbacks. If you
require further information or have any difficulty
obtaining them, write to: Mills & Boon Reader
Service, PO Box 236, Thornton Road, Croydon,
Surrey CR9 3RU, England.

*These two titles are available *only* from Mills & Boon
Reader Service.

# Mills & Boon
# the rose of romance

 **ROMANCE**

# Next month's romances from Mills & Boon

Each month, you can choose from a world of variety in romance with Mills & Boon. These are the new titles to look out for next month.

**NIGHT OF THE CONDOR** Sara Craven
**FORCE FIELD** Jane Donnelly
**IF LOVE BE BLIND** Emma Goldrick
**AN ENGAGEMENT IS ANNOUNCED** Claudia Jameson
**KISS OF FIRE** Charlotte Lamb
**INTIMATE STRANGERS** Sandra Marton
**TANGLED HEARTS** Carole Mortimer
**HIGH-COUNTRY GOVERNESS** Essie Summers
**CHALLENGE** Sophie Weston
**ELDORADO** Yvonne Whittal
*****SAVAGE AFFAIR** Margaret Mayo
*****TO TAME A WILD HEART** Quinn Wilder

Buy them from your usual paperback stockist, or write to: Mills & Boon Reader Service, P.O. Box 236, Thornton Rd, Croydon, Surrey CR9 3RU, England. Readers in Southern Africa — write to: Independent Book Services Pty, Postbag X3010, Randburg, 2125, S. Africa.

*These two titles are available *only* from Mills & Boon Reader Service.

## Mills & Boon
## the rose of romance

# A marriage for romance or revenge?

Twenty-one years ago Mario di Medici was murdered at sea. Many suspected it was James Tarleton's hand that had pushed him over the rail.

When his daughter, Chris Tarleton, came to Venice, the riddle of the past returned with her.

Before she knew how, she found herself married to Marcus di Medici, the dead man's son.

Was his marriage proposal intended to protect her from the shadowy figure that followed her every move?

Or was his motive revenge?

# ACCEPT 4
# MILLS & BOON ROMANCES
## ABSOLUTELY FREE

...after all, what better way to continue your enjoyment of the finest stories from the world's foremost romantic authors? This is a very special introductory offer designed for regular readers. Once you've read your four **free** books you can take out a subscription (although there's no obligation at all). Subscribers enjoy many special benefits and all these are described overleaf. ►►►